Sizzling

Triskelion Motorcycles Book 2

Robin Andrews

ROBIN ANDREWS

Sizzling

Triskelion Motorcycles Book 2

Robin Andrews

Published by STE Entertainment LLC

Copyright 2021 STE Entertainment LLC

Edited by AMR

Print Book ISBN: 978-1-7364606-3-4

All rights reserved. No part of this book may be reproduced, scanned, or distributed in any printed or electronic form without permission. Please do not participate in or encourage piracy of copyrighted materials in violation of the author's rights.

This is a work of fiction. Names, places, characters and incidents are the product of the author's imagination and are fictitious. Any resemblance to actual persons, living or dead, events or establishments is solely coincidental.

Table of Contents

Chapter One

Chapter Two

Chapter Three

Chapter Four

Chapter Five

Chapter Six

Chapter Seven

Chapter Eight

Chapter Nine

Chapter Ten

Chapter Eleven

Chapter Twelve

Chapter Thirteen

Chapter Fourteen

Chapter Fifteen

Chapter Sixteen

Chapter Seventeen

Excerpt from Blazing -Triskelion Motorcycles Book 1

About Robin Andrews

Other books by Robin Andrews

ROBIN ANDREWS

Author's Note

If you have followed my journey at all, you know that I had a long period where I just wasn't hearing from my characters at all. There was just so much going on in real life. Now, I kind of have the opposite problem. I have so many characters in my head that I'm racing to get it all on paper. But that's a good thing albeit a little stressful.

Through the good times and the bad times, I have had people that have still been there saying 'when are you going to finish this book?' and 'I need the next book'. To those people, thank you!

In the last six months I have discovered the joy of going to book signings as an author and I believe that has helped me feel the urge to write again. After all, if you see me at a book signing in April and then see me again in November and I have nothing new to offer, I don't look very productive. I am still struggling with pace. When I first started writing I released a book about every two months, and then I released nothing for months on end. Now I'm not sure where I'm going with number of releases in a year, but I figured that I will just write and when it's ready, it's ready. If I release two back to back and then nothing for a couple of months, that's okay. It's what my life allows right now. I'm still caring for my elderly parents and I am so thankful that my husband is at my side helping me with that. I wouldn't get much time to write if he wasn't.

Along my journey, I have met so many supportive people and have found that this community of authors and those who work with them is always there to lend a hand or give a suggestion. I know I wouldn't be where I am today without the support of family and friends.

This epilogue of this book is a bit of a teaser for the next major series I plan to begin after my current ones are done. But, more on that later. I hope you enjoy meeting Riley, Hannah and Maddie.

Chapter One

It was 8:00 a.m. when Riley met up with Deke, his partner for this assignment. They would have about an hour to discuss the schedule for the next couple of weeks, or maybe even months if that was how long it took. "Hey Deke." Riley said when his friend walked into Pops' Diner.

"Hey Riley." Deke said putting his hand out. When Riley grasped his hand, he was pulled into a one arm man hug. "We ready for this thing?"

"I think so, everyone is supposed to be meeting in the next couple of hours for the ride. I think we have a pretty good showing, pretty much the whole chapter is coming."

"Sounds good." Deke said taking the cup of coffee the waitress had handed him. "I'm sure you read the file." At Riley's nod, he continued, "This guy sounds like a piece of work. He was verbally and psychologically abusive to the mom as he was to the kid. She was too afraid to say anything. Thankfully, the school suspected something and got involved."

"Yeah, I can't imagine what the mom went through, but I'm glad it's over for them both." Riley said.

They finished their coffee and got ready to head out to begin the day. They would arrive about an hour before the rest of their chapter would ride by the house. Before they walked out the door, Pops stopped them with a greeting. "Hi Riley, Hello Deke. You two are here bright and early this morning."

"We have an assignment for BACA today." Riley explained.

Pops shook his head, "I don't know what gets into these monsters that so many small children get hurt. Children should be loved and cherished."

"You won't get any argument from us on that Pops." Deke said sadly.

Pops shook each of their hands and gave them a pat on the back when he said, "I'm with you in spirit, even if I am too old to take part in reality." They both nodded their understanding and headed out the door.

When they arrived, Riley knocked on the door, Deke standing slightly behind him. He was surprised at how pretty the mother of the little girl was. He had seen pictures of the little girl and every time he had looked at those, he couldn't get past the punch to the gut at how much her little brown eyes dug into his memories and to his very soul. But he hadn't seen pictures of the mother. She was a gorgeous petite woman. She had dark brown hair and the same soulful brown eyes that her daughter had. She was very obviously of Hispanic descent; her skin was a beautiful shade of light brown. "Hi, you must be Hannah." Riley said, giving her his best smile. "I'm Riley and this is my friend Deke. We're here from BACA".

She gave him a small smile; he could see the pain that she had suffered in her eyes. But she was doing her best to be strong for her daughter. "Of course, come in, please." She said opening the door wider. "Let me get Maddie." She went down the hall and came back a short time later with a little girl in tow.

Riley knew from the files that Madison Hayes was eight years old. When she looked up, she visibly shrank and hid behind her mother, obviously intimidated by the two men in her living room. They were both well over six feet tall, and had large muscular frames, and were wearing black leather jackets. They would be intimidating to pretty much anyone, but that was at least partially the point. They didn't want to intimidate Maddie, but they wanted her to see and feel their strength and support. That was a vital part of making this whole thing work, not to intimidate the little girl, but to be an intimidating force to the people who felt it was okay to bully those who were smaller or weaker than them. Riley knelt down on one knee so that he was at her eye level. "Hey, Maddie." He said with a smile. "I'm Riley, and this is my friend Deke. I want you to know that we are both here to be your friends and help you with going to court. We want you to know that we are here for you, and we will never hurt you in any way. We'd like you to become a part of our club."

The little girl peeked out from behind her mother and met Riley eye to eye. He made absolutely certain that she saw nothing but a smile and tenderness in his expression. That part of this was never hard for him because he felt it. He cared about these kids. He hadn't been one of the two to provide close cover before, but he had met several of the kids in the time he had volunteered with the group. Yeah, it was probably in part related to what had happened to him in Iraq, but he liked kids in general, he always had. He put out his hand, and asked, "We have a jacket for you if you want to be a part of our special club and everyone has a nickname in our club. We think your nickname should be Blaze. What do you say, can I get a high five?'

The little girl stepped partially out from behind her mother and leaned in to be able to reach his hand for a high five.

"Alright!" Riley said triumphantly. "I knew we were going to be good friends. Is it okay if we all go sit at the table, and we can tell you why we're here?"

The little girl looked to her mother and at her mother's nod, the little girl nodded too. They headed into the kitchen and sat around the table. Riley looked at the little girl and with the most sincerity he had ever had in his life, he said. "Deke and I are here to make sure that no one ever hurts you again. If it's okay with your mom, we have a cell phone for you." He looked at Hannah as he continued speaking. "The phone has a system that can be totally controlled by your mom. She can decide who you can call or text. She can decide what you can have on the phone. It's totally controlled by her." He pulled out a small simple flip phone, it was pink. When Hannah nodded her approval, Riley continued. "My number and Deke's number are already in there. We want you to be able to call us or text us at any time. If you have a bad dream, if you feel scared, or if you just want to talk, you can reach us right away." He handed her the phone.

Maddie opened it up and her mom showed her how to find the contacts. "See, there's Deke, and there's Riley. You just find the name of the person you want to call and hit the green button. Later we can put in other names too, like grandma and aunt Becca."

The little girl looked at Riley and smiled so he continued. "We mean it too; you can call us at any time. We are here to help you to feel safe. We will be with you every step of the way through this process. We will be in the courtroom with you, we will be here if you need us. Do either of you have any questions so far?"

Maddie looked a little timid, but she asked "why do you want to call me Blaze?

Deke looked at Riley and they both in unison sang "This girl is on fire." Maddie giggled at their antics and said, "But I'm not on fire."

Hannah said "No, Maddie, not on fire like really on fire. When a person is 'on fire' in the way they are talking about it means that she's awesome, she's strong, she's amazing." Maddie's eyes got huge.

Riley heard the roar of motorcycles in the distance. "Come outside with me for a minute." He got up from the table and reached out his hand, Maddie took his hand and followed him outside. "I want you to know that Deke and I are here to be your guardian angels, but I also want you to know that we have lots of friends that will be around to support you if you ever need anything. They wanted to come by today and see you." He pointed down the street as he saw the line of motorcycles slowly making their way down the road. There were at least seventy motorcycles, some with one rider, some with two. As each motorcycle slowly approached, they parked in long lines down both sides of the road. Each rider gave a smile and a wave to Maddie and her mom. At first the little girl seemed intimidated, but soon she was timidly waving back.

In awe, she whispered to her mother, "These people all want to be my friends?"

Her mother smiled at her and said, "Yes, sweetheart, so many people want to help you and want to be your friends. Riley and Deke will be our best friends, but all of these other people are here to help us if we need them."

That caused the little girl to smile broadly. "We have lots of friends, mommy."

"Yes, we do, Maddie, we sure do." her mother agreed. Riley could see the moisture in Hannah's eyes. It was most likely a huge relief to her to know that so many people were coming to her little girl's rescue after they had both suffered abuse at the hands of a man that Hannah had thought cared about her.

Maddie became more animated in her smiles and waves as she began to understand that this whole parade was just for her. As the last of the line of motorcycle riders walked up, Riley saw that the two bikes at the end held very familiar faces. When the group was all assembled, Deke pulled out the little vest that had been made just for Maddie. He addressed the group as he said. Members, we would like you to meet our newest addition to our group, this is Blaze." He held up the vest with the BACA symbol on it and the name Blaze embroidered across the chest. No one had worn helmets so it was far less intimidating for the child if she could see the faces of her new friends. They all applauded and sent up cheers. "Welcome Blaze" was heard echoing from all parts of the mass of people on the lawn. Each and every one of them, no matter how large, no matter how intimidating, had smiled at Madison that day and greeted her. They made her feel at ease with them. After the ceremony to welcome their new member was done the riders all got back on their bikes and slowly rode away, still waving and smiling at Maddie. Three people remained behind though. Riley embraced each of them. He turned to Hannah and Maddie and said, "These two men are my brothers, Bryan and Trevor, and this is my brother's girlfriend, Sophie."

Hannah shook hands with each of them and Maddie followed her mother's lead. When Sophie knelt in front of the little girl, she looked Maddie straight in the eye. "Hi, I'm Sophie, what's your name?"

"I'm Maddie" the little girl said shyly.

"Well, it's really nice to meet you, Maddie." Sophie said. "I just wanted to tell you, that you have the best of the best here. I was in a bind a few months ago. A really bad man was trying to hurt me, and Riley and his brothers here protected me and made that bad man go away. You can trust Riley to protect you from any bad people. I promise you that, I know I do."

Maddie looked up at Riley and then to his two brothers. "They made a bad man go away?" she whispered to Sophie

"They sure did." Sophie assured. "They chased him right away from me." Sophie wasn't going to say that the coward had tried to shoot Trevor and Riley had ended up having to shoot him to save his brother. Bryan had taken a bullet during the encounter too. The child didn't need to hear that, but she would gladly vouch for their ability to protect someone from the bad guy. From what Sophie knew, this little girl was almost nine years old and a man who used to be a neighbor had touched her in ways that were totally inappropriate. He had also threatened her to not say anything by promising to hurt her mother if she did. It had been a counselor at school that had figured out what was going on and had reported the incident to local law enforcement. BACA had been called in by the counselor. She was someone they had gotten recommendations from before and she liked the way the organization operated so she hadn't hesitated to call them in for this case. "I know that Riley and Deke are your guardian angels, but I promise you that I know Bryan and Trevor will be there if you need them too. And, if it's okay with you, I'd really like to be your friend." Sophie had the biggest smile, no one could resist that smile.

Madison looked at her mother and when her mother smiled, she looked back at Sophie and said. "I'd like that. Mr. Riley gave me a new phone, if it's okay, maybe I could call you sometime."

"I'd like that." Sophie said. "Maybe you and me and your mom could go out to lunch someday."

Sophie looked to Hannah and gave her a smile. She couldn't imagine what this woman was going through, it was something that no mother should ever have to face, but Sophie planned to lend support in whatever way she could.

"That would be great." Hannah said. "Would you like to come in for coffee?"

Sophie agreed and followed them into the house. She had a feeling that Riley might want to talk to his brothers. Around the kitchen table, the girls got to know each other a little while the men stood outside and talked.

"She seems like a really sweet kid" Trevor stated. "But are you sure you want to take this one, little brother?"

"Of course, I'm sure." Riley rebuffed. "Why wouldn't I? I volunteered, didn't I?"

"Yes, you did." Bryan stated. "And now that I see the girl, I have a strong feeling that I know why you signed up for this one."
"Is there something that I should know about?" Deke asked. "Cause if Riley can't handle this one, I think we need to find a fill in before they get any more attached."
"I can handle it just fine." Riley growled. "My big brothers here are worried that I signed up for this one because Maddie reminds me of someone that I knew from an op in Iraq."

"An op gone bad in Iraq." Trevor corrected.
"Yeah, okay, maybe when I saw her eyes, she reminded me of that day. But I want to do this, I'm ready to be a guardian angel. I've taken all the training and I'm ready."

"Okay, if you say you're ready, I believe you." Bryan assured. "And you know that Trevor is already monitoring her cell."

That was something that Trevor did for any of the BACA clients. "I know, it's basically just a simple flip phone so I don't think there's much to track, but it's always good to have an idea of location if needed." Trevor said and Riley agreed. They chatted for a few more minutes before going inside for coffee.

Chapter Two

Hannah had really liked Sophie and was looking forward to building a new friendship. It seemed that many of the people she had considered friends weren't so much what she had thought they were. Many had stopped talking to her. It wasn't fair, she and her daughter were the victims in all of this, but because they were standing up to fight, some people considered it too messy to be involved. While she was disappointed to have lost so many friends, she was glad that at least now she knew what their true colors were. Family had stood beside her; her family had always been close knit so she had no doubt that they would stick with her. But some of the friends had surprised her. She had thought that she knew them better. Oh well it was important that her daughter get justice and if that was too ugly for people then she didn't need them in her life. She would get herself and her daughter through this and see where life went from there. Maybe she should consider moving when this was done. She had lived in this neighborhood for almost a decade. Her husband had bought the small house for them when they got married. She loved the home he had picked for them. But with the scandal that had been brought on them by an unscrupulous neighbor, it might be time to find another place to go. Hannah wasn't sure she could afford that though. She didn't want to move her daughter to a small apartment where she would have no yard to play in, maybe she would just have to get used to the looks the neighbors gave her. She knew in her heart that they had done nothing wrong.

Riley could tell that Sophie's visit had meant a lot to both Hannah and Maddie. Sophie was one of those people that had a magnetic personality and a smile that warmed everyone. She had suffered her own torment at the hands of an abuser so she could relate to this situation. When his family had left, Maddie had asked to go out and play in the back yard. Deke had accompanied her. He had little brothers and sisters so he was hoping that he could win Maddie over. The yard was fenced in, and they really weren't too worried that the bad guy would make an attempt to enter the yard. He had a restraining order that was supposed to keep him off the property, but as Riley had learned those didn't always keep the big bad wolf away. And one of the notes in the file had said that some of the neighbors had been less than kind to both of the victims so it was time that they establish a presence for everyone to see.

Riley sat at the kitchen table with Hannah to go over what he knew about the case and see if there was anything else she could tell him.

"So, I know this isn't going to be easy, Hannah but can you give me the history of what led up to today?" Riley asked.

Hannah wrapped her hands around her coffee mug trying to absorb some heat from the porcelain. "Well, some of this goes back a long way but I think it all played a part in what eventually happened. I got married ten years ago to the love of my life. I was only seventeen, but I had completed school, so my parents gave their consent. Everyone in my family loved Hector. We knew each other forever. We grew up together. We moved into this house shortly after we got married. He worked so hard to buy this place for us." She paused for a minute to look all around her. It wasn't a big house, but it felt warm and filled with love. "He was in an accident on his way to work two years ago and he died. I was so alone for so long. My family tried to be there, but it's just not the same, you know."

Riley nodded "My parents died in an accident when I was ten. My brother Bryan that you met today, a friend of ours helped him get emancipated and stepped in as a guardian to help Bryan keep us all together."

"Is it just you three boys?" she asked.

"No, I have a sister, Summer. She's a tattoo artist, she has a shop right next to our motorcycle business." Riley explained.

Hannah nodded, "I have family and they really have been here for me, but when you have built a life with someone you love, it's just not the same. About a year ago, a new person moved into the neighborhood. He would stop by and offer his help. Small things at first, a board came loose on the steps, or a branch fell out of a tree. He would offer to help since he had noticed that no man lived here. At first, I thought that he was kind and observant, but now I know he was probably watching us for other reasons."

"I'm sure that it felt nice to have help." Riley encouraged. In no way did he want this woman to think that this could be her fault. She had done nothing wrong.

"Yes, and after a while, I started wondering if maybe he was interested in me, you know?"

"Fully understandable" Riley said. "You're a beautiful young woman who is available, why wouldn't you think that?"

"I was not ready for a relationship, but I admit it was nice having the attention. He was always so kind to Maddie and me that I started to accept his friendship and his offers of things. He would say he bought too much of something and offer for us to have it. He would say that if I ever needed someone to watch Maddie, he would be glad to." Hannah had tears in her eyes. "I never asked him to babysit, I just didn't feel right about that. But Maddie would be walking down the sidewalk and he would call her over to show her something. Eventually, he asked her to come into the house, always it was a new game, or something for her like a coloring book." She trailed off unable to continue at the moment.

"You don't have to go any further, I've read the police report, I know what happened from there. I wasn't trying to bring up painful thoughts, but it gives me a background as to what was going on that made him feel like he could approach you and Maddie." Riley stood and knelt beside her, he put an arm around her and assured her "You did nothing wrong, Hannah, it's human nature to want to have friends and to connect with people. He is just one of those people that have ill intentions but hide it behind the façade of a kind friend."

Hannah leaned into his shoulder and cried. "I was so wrong, I thought he wanted to date me, but what he wanted was to harm my daughter."

"I know sweetheart, I know." Riley consoled. "And we will do everything we can to make sure he gets everything he deserves." What Riley personally thought was that the guy deserved to be taken out into a field and beaten within an inch of his life. There was no justice harsh enough for someone who preyed on small children. But Riley wouldn't make things worse by committing another crime, he would just be the force to be reconned with if the guy ever showed up anywhere near these two.

Chapter Three

Later that evening when Maddie was sleeping, Riley and Deke sat at the table with Hannah to go over what the next couple of weeks had in store. "So, here's the plan." Riley began. "I know you've read the literature, but I just wanted to go over it and see if you have any questions." Hannah nodded so he continued. "You and Maddie have our phone numbers. I'm going to give you a list of other numbers too. Both of my brothers are on that list. My brother Trevor is a tech geek. He's already got location tracking on Maddie's phone. Since it's not a smart phone, he isn't tracking it for anything else. It's already got parental controls set so that anyone who you don't put in her approved list of contacts can't call or text her. I don't know how the perp would possibly get her number, but, even if he does, he can't contact her."

Deke continued with the details, "A lot of this is really up to you and what you want out of us. If you don't feel safe being alone, one of us will be here at all times. Or we can set up a schedule to work around your job and Maddie's school."

"Now that he made bail, I'd really like someone around when we aren't at work and school. I know he doesn't live in the house down the street anymore, but I don't trust him to not come by." Hannah said, she was rubbing her arms like she was trying to ward off a chill, even though it was late Summer.

"You've got it, whatever you need." Riley said. "I can stay here as much as you need me to. I work at a bike shop that my brothers and I own. And they are part of BACA too, so they totally understand. They've already told me that they have me covered at the shop until this is over.

Hannah was very happy to hear that. Both of these men were very large and very intimidating, if it weren't for the fact that she knew they were here for her and Madison, she would be afraid of them. "We only have the two bedrooms, but I can sleep on the sofa, and you can take my bed." she offered.

"Nonsense, I'm not putting you out of your own bedroom. I'm fine on the couch." Riley said.

Hannah was pretty sure that his muscular frame was quite a bit wider than her small couch, but she wasn't going to argue. Just having him in the house would be such a relief. When she had heard that her daughter's abuser was going to be released on bail, she had started looking over her shoulder and not sleeping much.

"You'll also find that there will be a broken down motorcycle in your driveway quiet often." Deke said. "Well, actually, it's not broken down at all, it runs great, but he won't know that if he drives by and sees me or Riley out there taking a bike apart." When she looked at him with a puzzled expression, he continued. "We like to make our presence known. If he does drive by, seeing me or Riley out there working on a bike might give him second thoughts about trying to stop in."

She got it now, they were going to make their presence known because there was no way that he would try to get to Maddie with one of these two on guard. The other neighbors would probably think it odd, especially since there would be two of them alternating, but she didn't care if they thought she was sleeping with both men if it kept her daughter safe. "I really appreciate everything you are doing for us; it really means a lot to me that men like you volunteer to help kids like Maddie."

"It's truly an honor for us to be able to help kids like this." Riley said.

Hannah thought she saw something cross his face, almost like he was haunted by something, but maybe she was just imagining it. She couldn't believe that a man like him had ever suffered any kind of abuse. Maybe he had just seen so much of it with his volunteer work with BACA.

When they were done with their coffee, Deke stood up and said, "Well, I'll head out for tonight. If you need anything you know you can call me. I'll be here in time to get Maddie to school." With that, he left.

"Are you sure you don't want to take my bed?" Hannah asked. "It's really no trouble, I don't think you will get much sleep on that little couch."

"That's okay, I don't usually sleep much anyway." Riley said. "I'll just rest a little. I'll try not to disturb you or Maddie though. I have headphones, I can watch a movie on my iPad or whatever."

"Okay, I'll go get you a pillow and a blanket in case you do get tired." she said as she left the room.

Riley made his way to the living room and got comfortable on the couch. He was pulling his iPad out when Hannah came back with the items she had promised.

"If you need anything else, my room is at the end of the hall. We usually get up by seven to get ready." She was still standing there for a few minutes.

Riley could tell that she had something on her mind. "What is it, Hannah? I can tell you're thinking about something."

"Oh, I was just wondering how this all worked. I know that Deke said he would be here to get Maddie to school. So, do you take shifts or what?"

"For the most part, we each work around one of your schedules, Deke has Maddie tomorrow so that puts you with me. I'll make sure that you get to work safely, and I'll be there when you get done. We suggest that you do whatever it takes to not have to leave work during the day. Pack a lunch or have one delivered or whatever. It's very unlikely that he would try to contact you at work, but if you went out of the building, well, we just don't know how persistent this guy is."

"Sophie told us how you and your brothers kept her safe from someone who wanted to hurt her." Hannah offered. "She told Maddie that she promises you will keep us safe."

Riley looked up at her, he could see a bit of worry in her eyes, but she was doing a fairly good job of trying to hide it. He looked her directly in the eye and said "I promise you, that someone will be with you and Maddie anytime you need us. That guy won't get within ten feet of either of you."

"You said that you own a bike shop with your brothers, so how is it that you were also keeping Sophie safe? she asked.

"Well, we do some PI and bodyguard type work too." Riley said like it was just another service the shop provided.

"Oh, so you're a hero then." Hannah said.

"No, I wouldn't say I'm a hero." Riley defended. "I have a lot of failures in my past, but I do promise you that I will do this job to the best of my ability and if at any time I think I'm in over my head, I'll call my brothers."

She smiled; she didn't know what he considered 'failures in his past' but she was pretty sure that she was right that he was a hero. At least he was one for her and Maddie. "Good night, Riley." she said, before she turned to go down the hall she added "Thanks for being here."

"Good night, Hannah. You don't need to thank me; this is all a part of what we do." He smiled at her as she turned to go to her bedroom. Riley went to the kitchen and heated up a cup of coffee. He was going to do his best to stay awake all night. The last thing he needed to do was fall asleep and have a nightmare. His dreams usually made him wake up screaming in a cold sweat, he didn't need to scare these girls any more than they already were. He would just crash during the day when Hannah was at work. It wasn't like he hadn't stayed up all night before, he could do it again and do it as often as he needed to so that Hannah and Maddie never had to hear his dreams. He took the coffee back to the couch; he propped the pillow behind his back and stretched his legs out on the couch. He probably wouldn't be able to sleep on this couch anyway. It was really small for someone his size. He put one ear bud in his ear, he let the other dangle. He wanted to be sure that he could hear any noises that might happen inside or outside the house. He started the movie he had been wanting to see on Netflix and settled in for a night of binge watching. Riley heard the shower shut off in Hannah's room and a few minutes later, he saw the light under her door go out. Maddie's room had a glow under the door like she probably slept with a night light on. He didn't doubt that had become even more necessary now that the big bad wolf had come knocking at her door. He would take great joy in watching that guy get sentenced to a long time in prison. People that preyed on innocent young girls like Maddie didn't deserve to walk around as free men. He had read the report, the guy was one sick bastard. Thankfully, he hadn't actually raped her, but he had touched her in ways that would haunt her for a long time. She was getting counseling, but he knew that even counseling didn't make it all go away. He had seen several shrinks over the years, and he still had nightmares of that night. He didn't let his mind go down that path though. His history was behind him, he needed to stay in the present and focus on protecting two very innocent females.

The following morning, Hannah cooked them all breakfast before Deke took Maddie to school and Riley followed Hannah to work. She had her own car, and they didn't want to take that freedom away from her if it wasn't necessary. Besides, Riley only had the bike he had arrived on the day before, Deke had brought a car so that Maddie could ride with him.

After Riley watched Hannah enter the secure building she worked in, He revved up his engine and headed toward the motorcycle shop. Deke had made arrangements with one of the other members to get a bike there that they could plant as something they could appear to be working on. Riley had thought about heading home to get a few hours of sleep, but he lived a way out of town and the shop was so much closer. He could grab a few hours of sleep take a shower and be back outside of Hannah's workplace before she was done for the day. At least he hoped he could get some sleep, that was a crap shoot for him most days.

"Hey Rye" Trevor said as he walked into the shop "What's up?"

"Just going to grab a few hours of sleep and a shower, Hannah's at work and Maddie's at school so they are both secure for now." he replied.

"Didn't sleep well?" Bryan asked.

Riley was pretty sure his brother was trying to dig for information as to the cause, but he wasn't going to volunteer anything. "Yeah, you didn't see the couch, not built for a guy my size to sleep." He saw the look that passed between his two brothers before he turned and made his way up the stairs to the small apartment. They all shared the responsibility of keeping it clean. Each had a few drawers and space in the closet where they kept an extra change of clothes or two. They never knew when a bike job would go long, or a security job might make it impossible to go home regularly. It had been one of the things that had made this the place they decided to buy. He took off his leather jacket and his shoes and fell onto the bed fully clothed otherwise.

He had an alarm set on his phone and to his surprise, he actually slept until it went off. He got up, took a quick shower, and realized that it had been hours since he had eaten. He grabbed a protein shake because he wasn't sure what the plan was going to be for dinner. He didn't want Hannah to feel like she had to feed him and Deke for every meal. He could tell by her home and clothing that she wasn't overly wealthy. The last thing BACA wanted for their clients to feel was obligated to spend money for their services. The group had ways of helping with food or things, but for now, Riley was just going to order pizza if everyone was okay with that.

He was sitting outside of the building Hannah worked in for about ten minutes before he saw her look out a window to make sure he was there before she left the building. When she walked out, she gave him a smile as she walked toward him. He was parked right next to her car. Damn but the woman was pretty. She was small in stature, but she wasn't waif thin. She had nice curves, definitely the look of a woman that he found attractive. He wouldn't move on his thoughts; this was an assignment and the last thing she needed was a man trying to start a relationship with her now. Maybe after this was all done, he would see if she would like to go out sometime. The group didn't have a policy against dating someone who had been a client. He just wasn't sure if he should try to start it while she was under their protection.

When they arrived at the house, Deke and Maddie were already there. His car was parked in front of the house. Normally, Hannah picked up Maddie at her after school program on her way home from work, but they had decided that it was best if Maddie not go to the program for the time being.

He got off of his motorcycle while Hannah parked her car in the garage. He went to the backyard where he heard the little girl playing. He gave a nod to Deke and then spoke to Maddie, "Hey Maddie, how was your day?"

"It was fun. Everybody at school wanted to know if Deke was my daddy. I told them no, he's my guardian angel. They all want their own now." She said with a smile.

Riley liked hearing that the little girl was looking at Deke as her guardian. That was the plan.

Hannah came out to the backyard and hugged her daughter. "I should go and see what I can find to fix for dinner." she said walking toward the house.

Riley didn't want to say anything about pizza out loud in front of Maddie until he knew whether or not she was even allowed to have pizza or if it was kept for a treat or something like that, so he followed Hannah toward the house. When they were almost to the door he quietly said "Hannah, I was thinking that maybe I could order a few pizzas for tonight. I'm sure you weren't planning on having to feed a couple of extra people, especially not people who probably have appetites like Deke and I do. But I wasn't sure if you and Maddie like pizza." He tried to keep it light because the last thing he wanted to do was make her feel like he was offering some sort of charity.

"Oh, that might be good. I can pay for it though; I don't want you having to spend your money for us. You are already doing so much." she protested. "I will have to go get groceries soon though I wasn't sure how this all worked and didn't think to buy extra food."

"Hey, don't worry about it. BACA has a fund set up for this type of thing. We realize that you aren't expecting to have to feed extra people and so that's part of what the fundraisers are all about." He wasn't going to tell her that he would be buying the pizza and most likely would pay for other things too. It was probably easier for her to accept if she didn't think it was coming out of his personal wallet. He wasn't wealthy, but he had a decent size savings from the military, and he made money in both of his careers.

"Okay, thank you." Hannah said she turned to her daughter and said "Mr. Riley is going to get us pizza for tonight. Can you tell him thank you, Maddie?"

"Pizza!" the girl yelled excitedly. "I love pizza. Thank you, Mr. Riley."

"You're welcome, but it's no big deal, I love pizza too and I'm super hungry." He was rather hungry. "What do you like on pizza?"

"I like lots of cheese and bacon!" she exclaimed.

"I'm afraid she's not overly adventurous when it comes to pizza" Hannah explained.

"That's no problem, I love cheese and bacon. What do you like on pizza?"

"Oh, I like almost anything except anchovies and mushrooms." she said.

Riley looked at Deke who just sort of shrugged his assent to whatever Riley wanted to order. Riley pulled out his cellphone and called one of his favorite local pizza places. "I'll take a large with extra cheese and extra bacon and a large supreme without mushrooms." He gave them the address for the delivery. "Just a minute" He turned to Hannah and asked, "Is pop okay or would you prefer something else?"

"I let Maddie have a glass of pop from time to time as long as it's caffeine free." Hannah stated.

He pulled the phone back to his mouth and said, "add a couple of two liters of Sprite or 7UP" He gave them his credit card number, if Hannah thought that odd, he would say that he would get reimbursed or something like that, heck, she wouldn't know if it was his card or one that had been provided to him by the organization.

They stayed outside enjoying the warm Spring Day. Riley wasn't sure exactly what the situation was going to be for Maddie having to be in court. Being as young as she was, she had already been videotaped and her testimony would be as minimal as possible in the actual courtroom, but the sixth amendment gave all criminals the right to face their accuser. The courts were pretty good about limiting the exposure of a small child, but he had learned over the years that it really was best to prepare the victim and have them testify and be questioned because it eliminated the possible loopholes that unscrupulous attorneys used to get a lighter sentence for their client. They would do their best to prepare Maddie for that day, and they would be right there with her when she had to point him out in court.

When the pizza arrived, they all sat around the kitchen table and ate. Maddie ate one slice; Hannah ate two and Riley and Deke finished off the two pizzas. Yeah, they were big eaters. After dinner Riley told Deke he could head out for the night, they were in and wouldn't be going back out. He would lock up and just hang out here. He knew Deke had some family; he didn't know all of the details though.

"You sure man? I don't mind staying if you want to go home. You stayed last night." Deke offered.

"Nah, I'd just go home to a big empty house, I might as well stay here so you can get home to your family." Riley said.

"Okay, I'll be here in time to take Maddie to school or Hannah to work, whichever you want to do." Deke said. He told Hannah and Maddie goodnight and headed home for the evening.

"So, Maddie, do you want to watch a movie or something?" Riley asked, and then he caught himself "If that's okay with your mom that is." He looked to Hannah.

She nodded so Maddie said "Do you wanna watch Moana? It's my favorite."

"Moana, I've never seen that one, but if it's your favorite, I bet it's awesome." Riley agreed.

Maddie went to put the Blu-ray in the player while Hanna turned on the TV.

Riley sat on one end of the couch and Hannah sat on the other, Maddie climbed in between them. She watched happily and sang along with the movie until close to the end when Moana had to face Te Fiti. She leaned over and wrapped her arm around Riley's arm and held tight leaning her head on his large tri-cep. She never took her eyes off the screen, she had likely seen the movie several times, but this part was still a little scary to her and she wanted someone to be there with her to go through it. Most likely she usually cuddled up to her mom, but apparently Riley had won over her respect as a protector and that was a very good thing. He didn't want to do anything that might give her a flashback or make either of them uncomfortable, so he just placed his free hand over her hand on his arm to reassure her that he was there, and he was on board with protecting her.

When the movie was over, Hannah said "Maddie, it's time to get ready to go to bed, go brush your teeth."

The little girl got up and started down the hall but turned to say, "Thank you Mr. Riley, thanks for watching Moana with me."

"If it okay with your mom, I'd like you to just call me Riley. I'm your friend, and even though I'm a grown up, I want us to be able to use first names."

Maddie looked at her mom and she shrugged. "Well, I think it's kind of silly to call a friend by something so formal. I know I usually teach you to call adults mister or missus, but in this case, I think Riley is fine."

"Thanks Riley" the little girl ran back and gave him a tight squeeze before going back to do as her mother requested.

"Thank you for that. I'm sure it wasn't the best movie you've ever seen, but it's her favorite and I know it meant a lot to her that you wanted to watch it with her. She'd become pretty reserved the last few weeks, which I am sure is normal all things considered. But it's good to see her starting to open up to people other than me again. Especially since you're a man. I wasn't sure if she would ever trust men again." Hannah said.

"Well, I'm glad I could help, and I really didn't mind the movie. It was kind of cool, I mean who doesn't love the Rock as an animated character?" he smiled at her. "I know your husband died awhile back. Has Maddie had any other men in her life? Have you dated anyone or anything like that?" As soon as he said it, he realized that it probably sounded wrong to ask her that, so he scrambled to explain. "I don't mean to pry, I just wondered how she's been around other men before and after what happened."

"No, I haven't dated anyone so other than my family, she hasn't really had any exposure to other men until you and Deke came along." Hannah said. "I really wasn't sure how this was all going to go. When I first saw you two, I had two thoughts. I thought here are these big men who will protect us, but I also thought that maybe Maddie would be scared of big men like you. But you are different, you are large, but you are so kind, and you seem to always get down on her level if you need to say something serious to her. Do you have children, Riley?"

"No, I'm single and don't have kids. I guess over the years I've been around a lot of kids in one way or another. But mostly I think it's because I lost my parents when I was young, you know?" he paused for a moment and then continued "I had some really great people in my life, my brothers and sister, and Pops of course. I think Pops really taught us a lot. When we were young, he would have us hang out at his diner or help with things. We all learned to cook and clean, he taught us that to make a family work, everyone has to do their share and be open and accepting of change."

"This Pops sounds like a really great guy." Hannah said. "I'd love to meet him sometime."
"Sure we can go out there some day. He makes the best sundaes. His burgers are pretty awesome too." Riley said.

"Well, I better go check on Maddie and make sure she brushed her teeth." Hannah said. She walked down the hall and Riley could hear the two talking. A few minutes later Hannah appeared in the hallway again. "Maddie would like to know if you would come and help tuck her in,"

"Sure, I can do that." Riley said. He followed Hannah down the hall to Maddie's bedroom. He stood just inside the door while the little girl said her bedtime prayers.

"Dear Jesus" she began "Thank you for letting us have my favorite pizza and watch my favorite movie tonight. Thank you for my new friends Riley and Deke. Please watch over Mommy and me and my new friends. Amen." She started to get up but bowed her head again and quickly added. "And Jesus, please let Riley be my best friend ever except for mommy."

Riley was blown away by the words of this small girl. He had hoped that she would accept him, but he was surprised that she had accepted him so much so quickly. When she hopped into bed, Riley walked over to follow her mom's actions. He didn't know how this whole tucking into bed thing went but he was happy to learn. Hannah leaned down and kissed her daughter and told her she loved her and wished her sweet dreams. When she was done, Maddie reached out her arms for Riley. He leaned over and kissed her forehead. "You have sweet dreams Maddie, and you don't worry about anything, I'm right out there in the living room if you need me, you just call me, okay?"

The little girl smiled and nodded and pulled her covers tight. "I love you mommy, I love you, Riley."

Riley didn't know what to say to that but in his mind, he knew right then and there that this little girl would never have to be afraid of anyone else again in her life. Even after the court case was over, he would protect her. It was what best friends did after all.

Hannah stepped out of the door with him and said, "I hope that was alright."

"It was fine, Hannah, kids are great, they say what they mean and it's a good thing that Maddie likes me and feels comfortable with me. That will go a long way toward helping us in this whole court situation." Riley explained.

"Well, it definitely means a lot to both of us to have you here." Hannah said. She would like to say more because she didn't think that was enough but there weren't words that could adequately say what she felt. "I'll let you get settled, are you sure you don't want the bed?" she asked.

"No, I'm fine out here, really. You go get some sleep." Riley offered.

"Okay, good night then." She made her way down the hall to the small bathroom to get ready for the night.

Riley took off his shirt and stretched. He needed to get some more exercise, or he was going to go soft on this mission. He could do push-ups and sit-ups pretty silently. If it weren't for the fact that he caught up on sleep during the day, he would hit the gym, but that was going to have to wait until this was over. He positioned himself in the middle of the living room floor and started doing push-ups as quietly as he could. He was about twenty in when he heard a gasp. He looked to see Hannah standing near him. Normally no one was ever able to sneak up on him, but he owed that to the physical exertion. He stopped and rolled so he was sitting on the floor. "Sorry, was I making too much noise?"

"No." Hannah said, she was just staring at him. "I've never seen your back tattoo before. It's amazing."

"Some of my sister's best work." Riley said. This was where things got awkward. People loved his tattoo, they wanted to see it, which wouldn't be so bad except for the fact that if they looked too closely, they saw what the ink was covering up.

"Can I see it?" Hannah asked. Then she realized that she was probably being rude. "Never mind I shouldn't have asked, that was rude of me. I just came out to tell you that there's plenty of room in the bathroom if you want to bring your toiletries or whatever, I can clear a shelf. Anyway, goodnight Riley."

He was pretty quick on his feet because she hadn't gotten fully turned before he was up and taking her hand. "It's not rude to ask to see my ink, Hannah. I don't mind. My sister does awesome work. She has done almost everything my brothers and I have except for a few small things they got while in the military. She has a shop right next door to our motorcycle place." This was where he had to tell himself no guts no glory. If he wanted Hannah to feel comfortable with him, he had to be willing to be vulnerable and let her see him, completely. He turned so that his back was under the bright light in the living room.

Hannah looked at Riley's back. The tattoo was definitely amazing. It was a long dragon that covered his entire back. When she looked more closely though, she could see small marks that looked like well healed scars. The scales of the dragon almost hid them, but not fully. Without realizing she was doing it, she reached out her hand to lightly touch his back. "Oh, Riley, it's beautiful." He flinched a little at her touch, so she pulled away immediately.

"Like I said, some of my sister's best work, you almost wouldn't know that my back looked about like hamburger at one point." He tried to sound like it was no big deal. He wasn't sure that he pulled it off.

"How did it happen?" Hannah asked softly.

"I was on an op in Iraq. I was carrying a small child away from a building when the building imploded or exploded whatever you want to call it. Most of the building collapsed in on itself, but small pieces of debris were splattered everywhere. I had seventy-eight pieces of building material in my back." He said it like he was just giving a report, eyes front, body straight, no emotion, nothing but just the facts. It had been years ago, the physical pain was almost never an issue unless he allowed himself to stay in one position too long, the mental stuff was still there but he had buried it deep except for when he was sleeping. Then he couldn't control his dreams.

Hannah couldn't help herself; she wrapped her arms around him from the back and pressed her head against him. "Oh Riley, you've always been a hero and protector of small children. You should be proud of all that you've done."

Riley wasn't so sure he would ever feel proud because so many had died that day, but he had always told himself that he had saved one person and that was a very good thing. He gently pulled himself out of her embrace so that he could turn to face her. He didn't want her to think that he was opposed to the way she had touched him. "Thank you for that. A lot of men died that day, so I haven't always felt like a hero, but I am thankful that I got at least one little girl out." He looked into Hannah's eyes and there was just something there, drawing him to her. He started to lean down to kiss her. Alarm bells were going off like tornado sirens in his head. This wasn't the time or the place to be kissing her, but he felt drawn to her anyway. He moved slowly so that she could absolutely pull away if she wanted to. She didn't though and soon, Riley connected with the softest lips he had ever felt. It wasn't a long passionate kiss, but there was a definite connection there. He held his lips to hers for a few brief moments and then pulled away. "I'm sorry Hannah, I shouldn't have done that" he said immediately.

"Riley, it's fine, I leaned in to meet you too. You didn't take advantage of me." Hannah said.

"Well, still I probably shouldn't have, considering the situation." he protested.

"Is there a rule against it?" she asked.

"No, it's not really a rule, I just don't know if it's appropriate." he said.

"Well, I didn't mind it and you weren't out of line. In fact, I kind of liked it" she stated. "I understand what you mean, this might not be the right time for us to start anything with all that is going on. But we're both adults Riley and I liked it, so don't feel bad, okay?"

"Okay." Riley agreed. He still wasn't sure that it actually was okay, and he for sure knew that it shouldn't happen again, but he didn't want her to feel bad about it.

"Good, have a good night Riley, and sweet dreams." She turned and went back to her bedroom.

Yeah, like he could have sweet dreams. He didn't plan on sleeping so that he could avoid his dreams. He usually tried to get just enough sleep to function but not so much that he wouldn't be utterly exhausted when his head hit the pillow when he could be assured no one was around. Sometimes the shear exhaustion kept the nightmares at bay, not always though.

Riley was awakened by soft voices down the hall. He had fallen asleep; he had not intended to let himself do that. But apparently it had happened anyway. On a good note, he hadn't had any nightmares, so he hadn't terrorized the whole house with his screams. If he were a superstitious man, he would say it was because Hannah had wished him sweet dreams or maybe it was because of that sweet kiss. Either way he had gotten a halfway decent night's sleep. He sat up and pulled his t-shirt back over his head and was getting up off the couch when Maddie came bounding down the hall.

"Hi Riley" she said with a smile. "Can you take me to school today?"

He was sort of surprised by the request although he realized he probably shouldn't have been. "Sorry, Maddie, I can't do that today. I only have my motorcycle here and I don't think that would be a good idea." He looked over her head to meet her mother's eyes. "But, if it's okay with you and okay with your mom, Deke and I can switch tomorrow. I'll have to go get my truck today after I drop your mom off."

She turned to her mother awaiting a reply. "That's fine with me. We can switch tomorrow if you want Riley to be the one to take you. Let's be nice in how we tell Deke though okay, I don't want you making him feel like you don't like him, understood?"

"Okay mommy" she made her way to the kitchen to wait for breakfast.

"You've definitely made an impression." Hannah said with a smile.

Riley chuckled a little and said, "I don't know if it was the cheese and bacon pizza or Moana though." There was a knock at the door, so Riley went to see who was there. It was Deke so he let him in. Quietly so no one in the kitchen would hear him he said "Apparently after watching a kid's movie and buying her favorite pizza, Maddie and I are besties now, so she wants us to switch off. I'll go pick up my truck today so that we can work it the other way tomorrow. Her mom doesn't want her to be rude to you about it though, so I wanted to give you the heads up. I know you don't care, but I think Maddie is going to feel awkward about it because her mom told her to be careful how she told you."

"Got it." Deke said softly as they started to walk towards the kitchen where their two clients were, he spoke a little louder. "Hey, man, would you mind trading off tomorrow. My car needs to go in the shop, and it would be nice to be able to ride my bike for a few days at least."

Riley gave him a nod of approval at just how smooth he was. "That's fine, I'll go get my truck today, so we're all set for tomorrow." As they walked into the kitchen, Riley saw the look Hannah gave him and he gave her a small smile and a wink.

"Hey kiddo," Deke said to Maddie. "I'm going to do the school run with you today, but I need to have some work done on my car so starting tomorrow, Riley's going to take you if that's okay with you."

Maddie looked at her mom with the biggest eyes as if she realized that her wish had come true without her having to do anything at all. She had the grace to accept it with humility though. "That's okay, I like Riley, so I don't mind. I like you too though." she said with a smile.

Chapter Four

When Riley met Hannah at work later that day, he followed her in his truck to the grocery store to pick up the things they needed.

"Would you or Deke want me to pick up any beer? I don't mind if you want to have one or two. I trust you guys to know what your limit is. I ask because I am planning to get myself a bottle of wine." Hannah asked as they walked around the grocery store.

"Actually, let me handle the beer." He said and pulled out his cellphone. "Hey sis, think I could get you to do a beer run for me?" Hannah was looking at him puzzled as he continued after a pause. "Yeah, but only you can get the good stuff. I'm on the assignment with BACA." After another pause, he said, "Great, Deke and I will appreciate it. I'll text you the address."

When he hung up the phone, Hannah jokingly asked "Are you a beer snob?"

"No, not really, but my sister has an in with one of the guys that owns Five Sloths Brewing. She's kind of dating him. So, she can get us some of the best microbrew in the city." Riley explained.

Hannah just shrugged and went back to her shopping. When they got home, there was a SUV in front of the house and Hannah could hear Maddie in the backyard. Riley carried all of the groceries in, he told her to go say hi to her daughter. He could put the things in the refrigerator and freezer, and she could show him where the other things went later.

When she stepped into the back yard, Maddie came running to her. "Mommy, mommy, come meet my new friends!" The little girl grabbed her by the hand and dragged her over to the chairs that Deke and two other adults were sitting in. "Mommy, this is Jeremy and Summer. Summer is Riley's big sister."

Jeremy stood and held out his hand, definitely a proper gentleman. "Hello, Mrs. Hayes, It's a pleasure to meet you."

"Please, call me Hannah." she said and then turned to the woman who her little girl was obviously enamored with. Maddie was sitting right next to Summer now and had a drawing in her hand. "You must be Summer. The tattoo you did on Riley's back shows amazing talent. It's beautiful."

"Thank you." Summer said.

"Look mommy, Summer drew me a picture of a mermaid." Maddie held up the sketch so her mother could see. "Isn't it pretty? Summer can draw really good."

"Yes, she can." Hannah turned back to Summer and said, "thank you for making it for her."

"It's no problem, I always have a sketch pad with me."

"And one in the bedroom and the bathroom, we usually have several on the kitchen table and counter" Jeremy said with a smile. It was obvious that he didn't mind them at all, he just wanted to tease his girlfriend a little.

"Well, what can I say, when inspiration hits me, I have to get it down on paper. It is my livelihood after all." Summer teased back.

Hannah got the feeling that this couple was very much in love. "Riley said you owned a shop right next to where he works."

"I do. My brothers helped me get set up there a few years ago when the building opened up. Have you met Trevor and Bryan?"

"Yes, they came with the group the other day, Sophie too." Hannah replied.

"I like Sophie, she is one of my new friends. She said she is going to take my mommy and me to lunch sometime." Maddie stated.

"Awesome, maybe we can all go sometime." Summer said. "I'd like to be friends with you and your mom too. If that's okay with you."

"I'd like that a lot. Some of our friends don't come over anymore so it's nice to have new friends." Maddie said. "I'm going to go swing now."

"If it's okay, I'll come and push you." Jeremy said. He looked to Hannah to make sure that was okay even though Maddie had whole heartedly agreed. Hannah nodded so he got up to go with the girl.

Hannah turned to notice that Deke was nowhere to be found at the moment, but she could still see Riley moving around through the kitchen window.

"Look, I'm a member of BACA too, and Jeremy is going to be soon, so we know sort of what's going on. We don't know the details because that's only told to the team assigned to the child, but if there is anything we can do to help, don't hesitate to ask. I know that people sometimes get awkward when they don't know how to handle a situation. When my parents died, pretty much everyone just didn't know what to do or say so they dropped off the map. We had a small but strong support group that helped keep us together, but yeah, people get weird sometimes with stuff they don't know how to handle. But Riley has all of us behind him and we're always willing to help when we can."

"Thank you, that means a lot to me." Hannah said softly. "Living in this neighborhood now is so hard. I see people all the time that used to call out to me and say hi or stop to chat while they are walking their dog, but now they just hurry on by or go the other way. It's like this has brought a stigma to the whole neighborhood. Some days I don't let Maddie come outside because people have said things through the fence. With Deke and Riley here, no one has had the nerve to say anything to her, but when they go, I don't know what we will do."

Summer had stood from her chair, and she rubbed Hannah's back soothingly and said "Well, you have a whole new bunch of friends and people that support you, so don't let them get to you. I know it's hard, but eventually they move on to the next piece of gossip or the next rumor and they'll leave you alone."

"That will be a good day." Hannah murmured.

Riley had put away all of the groceries and was looking out at the backyard. Deke had come in and asked if Riley minded if he headed out since it appeared everyone was in for the evening. Deke had a wife and a kid or two, Riley wasn't sure how many, but he had told the man it was fine to get home to his family. Hannah and Maddie were out there with Summer and Jeremy and though neither of them had his military training, they were alert and would make sure nothing happened. They would yell for him if anyone seemed to be hanging around the property. Summer had often been an extra set of eyes for them when he and his brothers had a bodyguarding job. He noticed how easy it seemed for Summer and Hannah to just talk like they had known each other for months not just moments. They seemed really comfortable with each other. Jeremy was pushing Maddie on the swing, and it was obvious that both of them were having fun. It seemed to him that Hannah and her daughter were the type of people that made connections easily and most likely before this situation had happened, they had probably had a lot of friends. It amazed him how people could turn on even the victims in a case like this because they didn't want to get their hands messy. He knew crap like that happened, but it shouldn't have happened to two really awesome people like these two. An idea came to him, and he picked up his cell to call his brother. When he answered Riley said "Hey Bryan, I wanted to run an idea past you. I haven't said anything here yet, so don't make it a concrete plan, but what would you think of having a cookout and letting Maddie come over to ride horses sometime this weekend?"

"That would be fine, just let me know what day and how many so we can figure out food and all that." Bryan replied.

"Great, I just get the feeling that with all that is going on, Hannah has lost some friends and even her neighbors are acting like she has the plague or something. It might be nice for them to get out of the city for a day. I'll let you know after I talk to her." With that he hung up and walked back out into the yard.

"Hey guys, thanks for bringing the beer over. I appreciate it. Deke had to take off, he had some family stuff going on tonight." He looked at Hannah and asked, "Can I talk to you for a minute?" He tilted his head to signify that he wanted to step away from the others to talk. When they were several steps from the others, Riley continued. "I was just talking to my brother Bryan. He was thinking about having a cookout this weekend and I told him I would see if you would like to come". Okay so that was a total lie, but it worked. "He lives out in the country, and he has horses. I thought it might be nice for you and Maddie to get away for a day, but I wasn't sure if you had other plans and I wasn't sure how you feel about horses. I didn't want to say anything in front of Maddie until I checked with you."

"No, we have no plans, and I am sure that Maddie would love to see the horses. But I insist on helping with the food." Hannah said.

"Yeah, sure, we usually have everyone bring a dish to pass or whatever. Bryan will take care of the main dish, burgers or steaks or whatever and then whoever comes brings a salad or something like that." Riley stated.

"That would be fine, just let me know what I can make. I am sure Maddie will love it." Hannah turned back to the others and said "Maddie, do you remember Bryan, the one who was here the other day?" the little girl nodded, she continued "He would like to have us over this weekend for a cookout, he has horses, would you like to do that?"

The little girl kicked her feet happily "I would like that a lot mommy, can we go please?" When her mother smiled, and nodded Maddie added "Can Summer and Jeremy come too?'""

"Of course, they can." Riley said, "They're part of the family." He looked at Summer and she nodded. So, the plan was made.

Chapter Five

The following day when Riley picked Maddie up from school, he got out to help her into his truck. It was pretty high for an eight-year-old girl. When he got back into the driver's seat, she giggled and said, "Guess what, Riley?"

"What?" he asked with enthusiasm.

"My friends asked me if you were my new daddy." she laughed.

"What did you tell them?" he asked.

"I told them that you weren't my daddy, but you are my new best friend." she explained.

Riley just smiled and nodded then started up the big truck. This little girl's pictures may have reminded him of that fateful day in Iraq but getting to know her was a happy thing for him. She was such a vibrant little girl despite what had happened to her. And she looked at everyone with such an open mind and an open heart. He was sure that was a tribute to the way her parents had raised her. In part, it may have been a detriment to her when she had met the neighbor that had taken advantage of her, but parents could only do so much to teach their children how the world worked. The rest of the ride home, Maddie told him all about her day and how she had told everyone that her new friends were taking her to see horses this weekend. She explained that some of them didn't believe her and some of them where anxious to hear about the horses.

The rest of the week was pretty much the same. Deke showed up and followed Hannah to work and then followed her home, one of the nights he had come in for dinner, but most of them he headed home to his family. Riley on the other hand was spending his days sleeping at Triskelion and his nights watching things on his iPad in the small living room of Hannah's home. They were seeming to fit together well. He helped with dinner if there was something that he could chop or mix while she prepared the rest, or he and Maddie played in the yard if Hannah had said she didn't need help because it was a simple thing. Riley really liked having home cooked meals though, he hadn't had much of that other than the few times he had been able to just happen to show up to take care of the horses when Bryan had been laid up. He knew about what time Sophie would be making dinner and he tried to plan his evenings accordingly. But Bryan was back to doing the work himself, so it had become more difficult for Riley to have an excuse to show up at dinner time. Now, he got a home cooked meal almost every night. It was something he was really going to miss when this was all over. He was going to miss Hannah and Maddie too. There wasn't a rule against him keeping in touch and he probably would to some extent, but they wouldn't need him to keep staying at the house with them. No, he was going to miss so many things about this when he had to go back to his normal routine. Other than the one night, there hadn't been any more kisses or anything with Hannah, but she often put her hand on his back when she was reaching past him or touched his arm when they were talking. He was starting to like this life more and more and he could see this type of a life in his future. Not necessarily with Hannah. But he definitely wanted a family someday.

When Saturday arrived, Maddie was so anxious for the outing for the day that Hannah could hardly get her to sit still long enough to eat breakfast. Finally, she had to tell her daughter that if she didn't eat, she wasn't going to get to go. That made the little girl sit and eat every bite of her cereal and drink her juice. But then she was ready to go, and it was still early. Riley looked over Maddie's head and mouthed to Hannah that they could go whenever, his brother wouldn't mind them getting there early. When Hannah nodded her agreement, Riley said, "You know what, maybe we should head over early. I'm sure Bryan and Sophie have a lot to do to get ready for all the people. Your mom and I can help them get ready and maybe you can keep Semper Fi out of everyone's way."

"Who's Semmer Fi" Maddie asked.

"No, honey, it's Sem- Per- Fi." her mother annunciated. "It means always faithful, or at least something close to that"

"Right," Riley agreed. "I haven't told you about Semper Fi? Well, she's one of the cutest little puppies I have ever seen. But she would be okay with you calling her Fi if that's easier, or Semper, we all just shorten the name down anyway."

"Bryan has horses and a puppy?" Maddie asked in amazement. "Oh, can we go now please mommy?"

"Okay, go grab your jacket in case it gets cold later and put on your old tennis shoes. Horses can be kind of dirty and you don't want to step in anything with your new school shoes." Hannah stated. The little girl ran off to follow her mother's command. "I think you are going to make her day with all of this. You'll be the best friend ever." Hannah said with a giggle.

"Well, it's a title I will wear with pride." Riley said. "I just figured that court will be starting soon, and she will need these fun things to think about during those long hard days. Thankfully, she doesn't have to be in the actual courtroom the whole time, but she has to be close by."

When Maddie came back out, they all climbed into Riley's truck and headed out into the country for a day of laughter and fun. Maddie asked about a thousand questions on the long drive out into the country. She asked about the horses, she asked about Fi. She asked about how big Bryan's house was and she asked if Summer would be there. All in all, she pretty much asked about anything and everything a child could dream of asking on a long drive.

When they pulled up to the house, Hannah was the one that was impressed. This was a massive farmhouse and while it was still styled to look like the hundred-year-old structure it was, it was very obvious that it had been updated and refurbished to have modern conveniences too. "This is a beautiful house" she said as they were getting out of the truck. She helped Maddie down from the high vehicle and she heard the door to the house open and a small ball of fluff came running down the steps.

"Semper, you be good." Sophie yelled. "Sorry, we're trying to work on training her, but she gets so excited when company comes over that the puppy in her just can't stay still."

"It's no problem" Hannah assured; her daughter was giggling wildly at the puppy who was kissing her all over her face. "Maddie doesn't mind, she likes dogs and this one is small enough that she can handle it. Thank you for inviting us to your beautiful home."

"Oh, you're welcome anytime. But I can't take much credit for the home, I've only lived here a few months myself, Bryan did all the work."

Just then Bryan stepped onto the porch and came up behind her and placed a hand on each shoulder. He leaned down and kissed her cheek and said, "But you made my house into a home, baby."

Hannah just smiled at them. It was wonderful to see people so in love. She had been like that at one point. Maybe she would find it again someday. She glanced over at Riley. Even though she had only known the man a few days, after the kiss they had shared, she had to admit that she was thinking about him more and more all the time. She knew that he was just being nice to her and her daughter because it was his assignment, but it would be nice if it could be something more. He seemed like a really decent guy and his family was amazing. Just from the short time she had been with his siblings and their partners, she could tell that there was a close bond between them. He would be the kind of man that would be loyal to his wife and children when and if he had them. Of course, she didn't even know if he wanted that out of life, not all men did.

They made their way into the house, Semper Fi had made a new friend for sure. The small puppy was just as enamored with the little girl as the girl was with the dog. She followed Maddie everywhere she went and although she had been taught not to jump up on people, it was obvious that she would gladly do so if invited. Her tail wagged so hard that her whole body moved.

"She's never been around kids since we got her, so I am sure she is loving this." Sophie said. "We got her from a family on a farm, so she was used to little kids."

"She's a great dog." Hannah said. "Maddie is totally taken with her."

As if to prove her mother right Maddie asked "Mommy, can I have a dog?"

"Not right now Maddie, we have a lot going on and we aren't home enough that a puppy would be happy." Hannah explained to her daughter.

The little girl looked disappointed until Riley chimed in and said, "We'll just have to come over here and visit Semper more often until things work out for you to get a puppy of your own." That put a smile back on her face.

"Would you like to come help me in the kitchen" Sophie asked Hannah. If Sophie wasn't mistaken, there was a look in the woman's eyes that said that maybe she had a thing for Riley. She certainly looked at him with longing in her eyes. When they got to the kitchen Sophie said "I don't really have a lot that I need help with, I just thought it might give us a chance to get to know each other better. Pull up a stool." she said pointing to the breakfast bar. When the woman was seated, Sophie continued "So how is it going having Riley stay at your house? I know it can be an adjustment having a stranger around all the time." She was hoping that was an open ended leading question that Hannah would take full advantage of if she had anything she wanted to share.

"It's been good actually. He ordered Maddie's favorite pizza and watched Moana with her the other night so apparently she thinks he is her bestie now." Hannah stopped as if she had realized she said something wrong. "Please don't mention that to his brothers, I don't want them teasing him about it"

"Well, I won't tell them although Maddie might, kids have a way of letting things like that slip out, but his family wouldn't give him a hard time over it, they would realize why he did it. They are all pretty great. They aren't going to give him shit for making her feel comfortable with him."

"You're right, I shouldn't have said that I just don't know them that well yet." Hannah said.

"No, I get it, and I can tell that you both really like Riley, so you just wanted to make sure he wasn't hassled, but I know the family and they get that he is doing what needs to be done to make Maddie feel safe and comfortable around him. They might give him some good natured teasing about things, but they would never really make him feel bad about what he does for Maddie." For some reason though, Hannah had a far off but sad look on her face. "Did I say something wrong?" Sophie asked.

"No, it's nothing that you said." Hannah explained. "I am so thankful to have Riley and Deke and all of you really to help Maddie through this whole court experience, but I hate to see her get too attached."

Hannah hadn't known it, but Riley had walked into the room from behind her. "Sophie, would you mind if I talked to Hannah for a minute?" he asked. Sophie shook her head, so Riley gently took Hannah by the hand took her out into a massive living room. "I think it's time that I shared a few things with you, sweetheart." he began. "First, no BACA assignment is ever over. We commit to helping them through court, but we plan to be a support for a long time afterwards. Secondly, even if that wasn't the group's policy, I wouldn't be going anywhere, I would never just walk away and hurt Maddie that way. And finally, that kiss the other night has been all I could think about. I've been cautious because I don't want to give Maddie the wrong idea of who I am, but I fully intend to ask you out on a date or whatever when it's appropriate to do so without it messing with what Maddie has to face in court."

Wow, that took Hannah by total surprise. Of course, she felt completely the same way. She would like to date Riley too at least to see if there was anything there. She had definitely felt a connection during their kiss, but she also knew that her life was not really in a place where she should be making decisions about a possible long-term relationship, and she should definitely be protecting her daughter from any more hurt. Not that she believed Riley would hurt her daughter, but if Maddie got too connected it would hurt if she thought Riley was going to be a permanent part of her life and something happened between the adults that made that not the case. "I'd like to see if we have a connection too, or date or whatever, but Maddie is my first priority in all of this. I don't know that it would work for us without Maddie getting into the middle of it and if it doesn't work out, "

"Hi," Sophie said softly from the doorway. "I didn't mean to overhear what you were saying but it was kind of hard not to from the kitchen."

"Sorry" both Riley and Hannah said in unison.

"Oh, don't be because I think I have the perfect solution to the problem. If Maddie has as much fun with the horses as she is having with Semper Fi, I think she would love to have a sleepover date sometime. That way you two could go out without her ever having to know that it was happening. You come and pick her up the next morning and she is none the wiser. If you are determined to keep her totally in the dark, when she is around, you are simply client and guardian angel."

Riley and Hannah both looked at each other considering her offer. Both were weighing out the pros and cons of that proposal in their minds. Finally, Hannah spoke "If Maddie is okay with it then I am fine with it too. Since the incident, I want everything she does to feel comfortable and okay for her. Not that I don't think you would take good care of her, but it has to be up to her."

"I understand totally, and I would suggest that we not say anything to her until later in the day. Right now, she is consumed with the puppy, but later she will have had time to get more comfortable with the house and with Bryan and I."

"That sounds like a good plan to me, how about you, Sweetheart?" Riley asked hopeful that Hannah would say yes.

"We will see how things go." she replied.

Riley could understand her hesitation, he didn't want Maddie to do anything she wasn't comfortable with either, but he really hoped to get a chance to take Hannah out for a date. He hadn't been lying when he said that kiss had stayed with him. The thing was it was a pretty ordinary kiss all things considered, but his mind didn't see it that way, nor had his body. He hadn't actually gotten aroused from the simple kiss, but if there had been a few more he would have easily done so. There was just something about Hannah that drew him in. He was sure that a part of it had to do with the fact that she was in a vulnerable situation right now. The protector in him had always been on the side of the underdog. Especially if the underdog was a woman or a child. He knew some would say that it was because of what happened that day in Iraq, but Riley would argue that point. His brothers hadn't had the same experience and they were both members of BACA and had opened a bodyguard service. It was ingrained in all three of them. Their father had always been like that too, he didn't have a lot of money and raising three kids hadn't been easy, but if he ever heard of a woman or a child that was in a bad spot, he would do what he could to help out. Riley remembered the lady that lived just down the street from them growing up. Her husband had died when Riley was a fairly young kid. Riley remembered his dad coming home from work and getting Bryan and Trevor to grab shovels and the three of them would go shovel out her driveway when a winter storm had hit. They hadn't really had a farm, but his mom had always had a nice garden. In the summer their dad would rototill out their garden patch and then head down the road to carve out a garden for Mrs. Sampson too. Really, they never thought much of it, it was just how things were in their household. After their parents had died, the older boys still kept up with helping the neighbor until she had decided that she was too old to live in that big old house all alone and had moved into an apartment somewhere near her daughter. When Riley realized his mind had gone down a long rabbit hole, he focused back on the two women and said. "Right, we'll see how it goes and if she isn't comfortable with it, I have no problem waiting but I do want to date you Hannah, whenever the time is right. Are you ready to head outside?" At her nod, he placed a hand at the small of her back and led her out on to the huge deck at the back of the house.

Hannah was enjoying the meal with Riley's family. She felt like she had known them for years rather than just a handful of days. They were so easy going and seemed to accept everyone with open arms. Maddie had complained that she had to quit playing with the puppy to eat, but Riley had stepped in and told the little girl that the sooner they got their food gone the sooner they could ride the horses. She had immediately taken her place at the table. Apparently, the puppy was already enthralled with the small child. While they ate, Sempre Fi sat curled up by Maddie's feet. The puppy was well behaved though and didn't try to interrupt the meal or beg food off of anyone, it had obviously been well trained.

When they finished eating, Hannah helped Sophie clear the food and put away leftovers. They had started with a lot of food but there wasn't a whole lot left. Riley and his brothers could definitely eat, of course they were big men. Riley asked Hannah if she was okay with him taking Maddie out to the barn to show her the horses. She appreciated that he didn't just assume it was okay. She had become a protective mother hen even more than she had been before. She trusted Riley completely with her daughter, but it was still good that he always asked rather than assumed she would be okay with him taking her daughter somewhere.

By the time she and Sophie got out to the barn, Maddie had picked what horse she wanted to ride. "I like the gray one, mommy. Her name is Stormy, can I ride her, please mommy?"

Hannah looked at Riley to see what he thought of that idea. She had no doubt that he would steer Maddie to a different horse if he didn't think that one had the right temperament for a small child.

When Riley noticed Hannah's look, he said, "Here Maddy, let me get a saddle and you can ride in front of me if that's okay with your mom."

Hannah loved how he never made a commitment to the little girl, he always said it was up to her mom. "That sounds fine to me." She said. "Maybe I can get a turn too."

"Do you want to ride by yourself or with someone?" Riley asked.

"Um, maybe with you when you get back, at least for the first time anyway. I don't know the first thing about horses." she explained.

"That's no problem, I can come back and give you a turn, or if Maddie wants, she can ride Stormy with Sophie and you and I can ride another horse." Riley offered. He looked to Maddie to see what she wanted to do.

"I can ride with Sophie mommy, that way you can ride too." Maddie said. "I want to go for a long, long ride and I don't want you to have to sit here waiting."

Riley was so glad Maddie felt that way. He wanted to go for a long ride on the trails behind Bryan's house and having his arm wrapped around Hannah while she sat in front of him would be almost as good as having her riding behind him on his Harley. He put the saddle on Belle, one of the chestnut horses while Bryan saddled up Stormy for Sophie and Maddie. He saddled up a horse for himself too. Trevor, Summer and Jeremy were going to stay back at the house. Bryan didn't have enough horses for all of them anyway.

Riley showed Hannah how to put her foot in the stirrup and he helped her onto the horse in front of him. Since the saddle was really only made for one person, Hannah was more in his lap than in front of him really and he did not have a problem with that. He knew that he had to be careful, there were watchful eyes on them, but he could hold her to him and take in her softness and her scent. He definitely hoped that Maddie would be okay with doing a sleep over with Sophie sometime. The sooner the better.

Before they headed out of the barn Riley leaned in to speak softly in Hannah's ear. "I seriously hope that I don't offend you with this Hannah, but I'm pretty sure I won't be able to keep myself from getting at least a little aroused with you sitting so close to me like this."

Hannah blushed a little but told him that she understood. As they rode along the trails, Bryan took the lead when the path was more narrow. Sophie followed behind him and Riley took up the rear. Maddie was constantly pointing out some bird or flower or small animal as they made their way through the woods. Bryan took the longest of the trails so that Maddie could have the full experience.

Riley didn't mind that at all. He liked having Hannah in his lap and being behind Maddie for parts of the trail offered him the opportunity to sneak a kiss to Hannah's cheek or nuzzle in her hair. He also got a chance to get to know her more. They had talked some before, but this gave them an opportunity to chat without an audience.

"What do you think would be a fun first date, Hannah?" Riley asked. He kept his voice soft so that Maddie wouldn't hear him although it was unlikely that she would hear much with her excited babble about the horse and the surroundings as well as her hundreds of questions for Sophie.

"I don't know." Hannah began. "I'm pretty simple really, we don't need to do anything fancy. I like getting to know you and I have done that some already, but there is only so much we can say with little ears around. So, it would be nice to just be alone. I can even make dinner at my house."

"No, sweetheart, if I date you, I don't want to make you have to cook. I don't want you to have to work, I want it to be fun for you." Riley said. "What types of things do you enjoy?"

"I like the water, swimming, boating or just being on the beach." She began. "I like most types of food; I like quiet walks in the park or going to farmers markets and fairs. I'm pretty flexible on things to do."

Riley didn't admit that for a second when she had said flexible his mind had gone in a whole other direction. "That's good to know sweetheart. I will plan something fun for us if this works out."

Hannah really liked it that Riley called her sweetheart. It was a nice feeling to be someone's sweetheart. It had been a long time since she had felt special to anyone. "It's really no pressure, I'm happy just to spend time getting to know you." she assured.

Riley decided that there was no time like the present to start to get to know each other better so he suggested a game of sorts. "How about we start now. I'll ask you a question and give you what my answer would be to that question then it's your turn. For example, I could ask what's your favorite color. My answer would be blue, what would yours be?"

"Purple" she stated.

"Now it's your turn." Riley encouraged.

Hannah thought for a minute but then asked "What's your favorite movie? Mine is Notting Hill."

"Well, besides Moana" Riley said with a chuckle, "I like Conspiracy Theory".

Hannah giggled. "Well, of course, who doesn't love Moana? But I've never seen Conspiracy Theory." Hannah said.

"We'll have to rectify that then." Riley stated. "What's your favorite flower? Mine is an Iris because my mom used to grow them all around our house."

"I like lilacs and hyacinths because they both can make a whole yard smell pretty." Hannah replied. "

Riley smiled down at her, sometimes things just happened to work out well. "I'll have to take you to my house sometime then." he stated. "I bought a house that has a whole row of lilacs along the property line."

"I'll bet that smells amazing in the Spring." she exclaimed. Their game was interrupted by Maddie.

"Look mommy, look Riley." she exclaimed. "There's water!" They had come to a small stream that ran through the woods. It wasn't deep and the horses could easily walk right across it.

"Maybe you can come and swim sometime." Sophie encouraged. She looked at Hannah, "It's not deep, barely to my knees, but Maddie might have fun with it. Bryan is a trained lifeguard, so you wouldn't have to worry about her."

"Can I mommy, can I?" Maddie begged.

Hannah had to give it to Sophie she was obviously determined to give them a chance to get away for a date. "Probably sweetie, we'll have to see when it works out."

Maddie squealed with excitement as the horses just kept going like the water didn't bother them at all. They were quiet for a bit but then Riley encouraged "I believe it's your turn, unless you are tired of the game."

"No, I have a hard time thinking of questions." she explained. "Give me a minute."

"It doesn't have to be a favorite question, you can ask me anything, Hannah. I'll be completely honest with you." Riley offered.

Hannah had no doubt that would be true. "How long have you been with BACA?"

"I've been with the group for a couple of years although this in my first time being one of the two that are assigned directly. Bryan and Trevor have been with them longer than I have." He hesitated for a minute but eventually he continued. "I don't know, it took me a while to be ready, I guess. When I first got home, I had lots of injuries both visible and not. I had to get my body and my head where it needed to be before I could take on something like this. If I hadn't had my family and Pops, I don't know where I would be. I'd probably have relied on a substance of some sort to get me through it. Actually, I started to with the pain pills they gave me. It would have been so easy to get hooked on. But my brothers came along and kicked my ass and told me to man up. Don't get me wrong, they were all for me taking them if I needed them, but they weren't going to let me use them as a crutch. And I easily could have used them that way. Honestly the physical pain wasn't bad after the first month or so, but the mental pain would have crippled me if it hadn't been for family."

He was quiet for a moment and Hannah almost felt like she should say something to comfort him. He started speaking again though. "When I turned around and saw that building a pile of rubble, I knew that my entire squad had to be dead. By the time they got done with clean up, I was the only one alive, they found everyone except one other guy, and he was considered missing presumed dead. I still to this day can't say that I understand why I was the one to make it out alive. There was a lot of guilt for a while. I mean why me? Why did they all die, and I lived. I went through a phase where I just wished I had died. But my family wasn't going to let me get away with that shit. They thought they were clever, but I knew what they were doing. Someone was always coming over or needing my help with something. They didn't let me sit and dwell on it much. Bryan made me learn how to fix motorcycles and gave me a job at the shop. Summer got started on my tattoo as soon as the skin was healed enough and trust me, that took a lot of hours. She talked to me incessantly, she never forced me to talk about that day, but she never let me get into my own head."

This time when he stopped, Hannah had watery eyes. "Riley, I don't know exactly why you didn't die that day, but I'm glad you didn't. Maddie and I wouldn't have gotten a chance to know you if you had."

Riley squeezed her a little tighter to him and they rode in silence for a while. Well Maddie was still chattering away about everything she saw, but the adults were quiet.

When they got back to the barn, Maddie wanted to help brush down the horses, so Riley showed her how. He picked her up and helped her to be able to reach. Hannah stood back and watched Riley with her daughter. He may not have kids, but he was really good with them.

Sophie watched Hannah watching her daughter and Riley. She was pretty sure that there was going to be something going on between the two of them soon if there wasn't already. She would be glad to see Riley happy. He would be a great stepdad too. He was such a protective and caring person. All of the Lawson's were, but Riley seemed to be the most tender hearted of them all.

When they got back to the house, they all sat around for a little while talking but eventually, Hannah said "we should probably head home, I need to get Maddie some supper and bedtime isn't far off."

Maddie groaned, "But mom, I don't want to go home, I like it here."

"Well, we definitely need to plan a sleep over sometime then." Sophie said. "Maybe next weekend, if your mom thinks that's okay."

"Can I mommy?" Maddie said rushing to her mother's side. "Please"

"You haven't ever spent the night with someone by yourself. Are you sure you're ready for that?" Hannah asked.

"Mooommm." the little girl said with exasperation, "I'm almost nine years old. Of course, I'm ready."

Hannah sort of chuckled but said, "Okay, probably. We'll see if you still want to by Friday, we'll call Sophie and make plans." She didn't say it, but the adults all knew that the trial was starting this week and while Maddie wouldn't have to be in the courtroom for most of it there was a chance that they would get to her testimony by mid-week.

Jeremy pulled Riley aside and said, "I wanted to talk to you about something."

"What's that?"

"Well, I am fairly new to this whole BACA thing, so I don't know how things work, but I do have some sway with the legal system between my dad being a senator and the Five Sloths guys. I was wondering if you thought it would be a good idea to stage a mock testimony for Maddie. I'm sure we could use an empty courtroom for an hour or so. We could all take a role in it and show her basically how the day would go. Show her where the perpetrator will be sitting, where you guys will be. It might help her feel more comfortable if she has an idea of how things will go."

Riley thought about that for a minute. "That sounds like a really good idea. You see what you can work on your end and let me know."

"I'll do that." Jeremy assured.

Hannah thanked everyone for the fun day and told Maddie to do the same. With one last puppy kiss from Sempre Fi, they were ready to go.

Chapter Six

Riley offered to swing through a fast-food place on their way home it would make it quicker and easier than Hannah having to cook. Hannah agreed that it would be easier after a long day although she didn't like to take Maddie for fast food very often.

By the time they reached Hannah's home, Maddie was exhausted from her long and exciting day. She brushed her teeth and was ready to say her prayers without any objection at all. Again, she asked Riley to help tuck her in too and again he was in her bedtime prayer. This kid was tugging on his heartstrings with all she had in her.

After she was all tucked in, Riley asked Hannah if he could speak to her for a moment. He wanted to run Jeremy's idea past her. He didn't want to do anything that Hannah didn't feel was in Maddie's best interest. When they got to the kitchen he began "So, Jeremy came up with an idea and I think it sounds good, but I wanted to make sure you were okay with it. "If you're not, I totally understand, and the conversation will be dropped." When Hannah gave him a nod of her head he continued "His idea is to try to take Maddie into an empty courtroom so that she can get a feel for the lay out. We can see if we can get my family and maybe some of Jeremy's friends to role play a little. We won't talk about what happened to her at all, but we will show her where the judge sits and how Deke and I will be right behind the bad man."

Hannah thought about that for a while. It did kind of sound like a good idea. "Jeremy can arrange all of this?" she asked.

"Yeah, his dad's a big shot Senator and most of the guys at Five Sloths are lawyers so he can probably find out when a room will be empty and get permission to use it for an hour or so."

"Yeah, I think it would be good, as long as Maddie is okay with it" Hannah agreed.

"Great. We'll see what we can work out."

Before she headed to bed, Hannah told Riley "Thank you for a wonderful day. I know Maddie was over the top happy with being able to go and I enjoyed it a lot. Your family is amazing."

"It's no problem sweetheart. I'm sure you'll be seeing more of them in the future."

"Well, anyway, I had a good time." She stood up on her tip toes and kissed Riley on the cheek.

Riley didn't let her pull away from him, he held her in place and leaned in for a real kiss, not just a peck on the cheek. "I had a good time too Hannah. I'll take you horseback riding anytime, and I am looking forward to getting a chance to take you for a ride on my Harley someday too." He kissed her deeply and she responded just as passionately. They stood there kissing for a few minutes before Hannah pulled away and Riley let her.

"I know Maddie is probably down for the count, but I just don't want to take a chance on her seeing us until this trial is over and we have a chance to see if we are compatible. I don't want to confuse her." Hannah explained.

"I know, and I feel the same way. It's not a problem sweetheart." he assured. "You have a good night."

"You too, Riley. Sweet dreams." She gave him one more quick kiss and then went to get ready for bed.

Riley got his pillow and laid on the couch. He hadn't gotten a chance to take a nap that day, so he was really tired. He just had to hope that the whole theory about not having bad dreams when Hannah wished him a goodnight was accurate because there was no way he was going to be able to stay awake all night.

****

Apparently, the theory was gaining more validity because he slept through the night again. It was a lazy Sunday morning around Hannah's house. Riley made the suggestion that they take a drive out to Pop's Diner for lunch, and everyone agreed.

When they arrived at the diner, Pops greeted them with enthusiasm. "Riley, it's good to see you again so soon! And who have you brought with you?"

"Pops, this is Hannah, and this is Maddie." Riley said.

"Oh my, two lovely ladies have graced my diner today." he exclaimed. "It's so good to meet you both!"

"It's nice to meet you too." Hannah said extending her hand. Maddie just looked at him and smiled.

After shaking Hannah's hand, and giving Maddie a wink, Pops showed them to a table. "One of the waitresses will be right with you" he said after handing them menus. "If you don't mind, I'll come back after you have a chance to order so I can get to know you a little."

Riley knew that Pops knew exactly who his guests were. He would easily put two and two together and know this was Riley's

BACA assignment. Pops loved everyone he had ever met and always treated everyone like they were a long lost friend.

Maddie asked if she could have ice cream for lunch and Hannah told her she could have some for dessert if she ate her chicken tenders first. The little girl was slightly bummed but agreed that that was okay.

When Pops came and sat next to Riley in the booth he asked "So, Maddie, how old are you?"

"I'm almost nine." she said with pride.

"Wow, really, that's such a good age to be." the older man exclaimed. Riley didn't miss the brief glance that Pops gave him that spoke volumes about his thoughts on someone having taken advantage of this small child.

"Uh huh. I got to ride a horse yesterday. Pretty soon I'll be old enough to ride one all by myself. But yesterday I rode with my friend Sophie." she explained.

"Oh, you know Sophie and Bryan?" he asked.

"Yes" she said very seriously, "they are all my friends, but Riley is my best friend."

"Riley is a good best friend to have." Pops agreed.

"Uh huh, he saved Sophie from a bad man and he's going to do the same thing for me." she said confidently.

"I have no doubt that he will, Maddie, he's very good at that." Pops turned to Hannah and asked. "And what about you, my dear, tell me about you?"

"Well, I work as an administrative assistant for Kellerman's. I've lived in Grand Rapids my whole life. I don't really know what to tell you about myself."

"Do you believe that Riley will keep you both safe from the bad man?" he asked.

Hannah took a minute to look Riley in the eyes and said, "Without a doubt." The look that she gave him showed her trust and maybe a something a little more like desire or connection on a different level. He just smiled back at her.

While they had been talking, they had also been munching on their food and had cleared their plates for the most part. Maddie asked, "Can I have ice cream, Mommy? I ate my chicken."

"Yes, you can sweetie."

"Then I shall go and make three of my special sundaes." Pop said.

"I've heard they are a legend." Hannah said.

Pops just smiled and winked at the two females as he got up to head to the kitchen to make their treats.

"I can see why he does so well with this diner. It's really kind of out of the way for most people to want to come. But the food and atmosphere is great and Pops himself is a big part of why people keep coming back." Hannah said.

"I like him, he's nice." Maddie agreed.

They ate their sundaes and visited with Pops some more before getting ready to head out. Just before they left Riley got a text from Jeremy.

Everything's set for four o'clock tomorrow. Meet me at the courthouse entrance. Bring whoever you think should be there.

Sounds good. Thanks for taking care of this.

Hannah had noticed Riley texting with someone, but she had no idea who it was. When he caught her looking at him, he explained "Something I need to tell you about later." He kind of shifted his eyes to Maddie and then back to indicate that it wasn't something he wanted to say in front of her. Hannah just nodded.

When they got back to Hannah's house, Maddie went to play in the backyard and Hannah and Riley sat on the back patio. "The text I got was from Jeremy. He has it all set up so that at four o'clock tomorrow we have use of a courtroom. It may not be the exact courtroom, but they pretty much all look the same. We can take Maddie in there and show her where people will be sitting and give her an idea of how things will go. If you think that sounds like a good idea."

"It can't hurt, I don't know if it will help, but it can't hurt. Do you know how much she is going to have to say in front of everyone?" Hannah asked. She looked worried about what her small child would have to face.

"I don't know for sure. I do know that the younger the child, the less they actually make them have to say in front of the courtroom. Sometimes the judge takes them to his chambers, or sometimes they do most of it on video. I don't think she will have to go into details in front of everyone, but I can't promise that for sure."

Hannah just nodded sadly. Riley put an arm around her and gave her a squeeze, he wanted to take her in his arms and hold her until she felt better, but Maddie was only a few yards away.

"Do you think we should tell her about it now or wait until we are headed there tomorrow?" Riley asked.

"We'll tell her tonight before she goes to bed." Hannah said.

Riley liked the way she talked about them as a 'we'. He was feeling more and more like he wanted to be a part of them for a long time. He hoped Hannah and Maddie would both feel the same. He had no doubt that Hannah wouldn't break things off with him if it became a problem for Maddie. And that was understandable, he wouldn't want it any other way.

That night when they tucked her in, Hannah told Maddie "Riley and Jeremy worked out a plan that I think might be a good one." Maddie just looked at her trustingly. "You know that I have told you that sometime soon we will have to go to court and talk about what the bad man did to you, right?"

Maddie nodded and Riley didn't miss the fear in her eyes.

"Well, tomorrow after school we are going to go to the courthouse" Maddie visibly tensed up and Riley instinctively took her hand in his. "it's not for the real time. This one will be pretend, just so that you can see what it looks like and where people will sit and all that. No one will be there except us."

"Will my friends be there?" she asked.

"Definitely me and Deke and Jeremy for sure," Riley stated. "I'll see if anyone else can make it okay?"

She just nodded. They finished the normal bedtime rituals and Riley told her one other thing before kissing her on the forehead goodnight "The bad man won't be there tomorrow Maddie and on the day that he is there, no one will let him get anywhere close to you. I promise you that." Maddie gave him a small smile and wrapped her arms around his neck and hugged tightly for a long while.

When they were standing outside of Maddie's closed door, Riley drew Hannah into him and held her tightly. She fit so perfectly against him, her head falling solidly over his heart. "She'll be okay Hannah. I promise, we will make sure she is okay, no one is ever going to hurt her again."

Hannah just wrapped her arms around his waist and said, "Thank you."

"No thanks necessary, sweetheart. I would do it gladly for any small child. But you and Maddie are both special to me. We'll get through this and then we can see what the future holds." Riley assured.

They stood embracing each other for several minutes but when Hannah pulled away enough to look into Riley's eyes, he leaned in and kissed her. He wasn't going to push her to make it any more passionate than she wanted it to be. If she pulled back after a brief kiss, so be it. When she didn't pull away but pressed in further Riley pulled her closer to him. Finally, his brain registered that they were standing right outside of Maddie's door and while he was pretty sure he would hear her if she got up, he didn't want to take any chances. He scooped Hannah up and for a brief moment, he thought about carrying her across the hall to her bedroom, but he didn't want to rush her into anything so instead he carried her to the sofa in the living room. He sat down with her across his lap and put his hand behind her head. He looked into her eyes and said "Hanna we won't do anything you aren't comfortable with tonight or any other time that we are together. I am fine with just sitting here and holding you for a while or kissing you. I am pretty sure Maddie is down for the count, but I also have pretty sensitive hearing thanks to my military training. If I hear her move at all, I will set you aside and she will never know we aren't just sitting here talking. But if it's okay with you, I'd like to keep you right here for a while."

Hannah loved the fact that Riley always gave her a say in anything that happened with her. He didn't just expect her to comply with whatever he was doing. She had absolutely no objection to sitting on his lap and kissing him. She trusted him when he said he would stop if he heard Maddie moving around. "I'd like that too." she said with a smile.

Riley used his hand on the back of Hannah's head to draw her to him. Her shirt had ridden up slightly and a small area of skin was exposed above the waistband of her pants. Riley gently rubbed his thumb across her soft skin while they kissed, their tongues doing a dance that was beyond erotic. Between kissing her and touching her soft skin, Riley was getting very aroused.

Hannah couldn't believe how easily this man could arouse her so fully. He wasn't even touching her in any sexual way. He was simply running his thumb over the skin of her abdomen and kissing her and yet she was wishing for so much more. She knew that they couldn't do more because as good as his hearing might be, she wouldn't take a chance on Maddie walking in on that. She could feel his hard cock under her, and she briefly thought about turning herself so that she could straddle him but if she did that, she wasn't sure any of them would be able to stop. Finally, she made herself pull away and Riley didn't hesitate to allow her to. "I think I better get to bed, if I stay here much longer, I don't think either of us is going to want to stop."

Riley moved both of his arms away from her and agreed "You're probably right sweetheart. I hope we can pursue more of that when we can be alone."

Hannah smiled and kissed him quickly one last time "Good night Riley, sweet dreams"

"I'm pretty sure my dreams will be more steamy than sweet, but thank you Hannah, Good night." Riley said. He waited until she was done in the bathroom before he headed down there to take a shower and get ready for bed. He turned the dial way colder than he usually did.

Just before laying down for the night, he sent a group text to his siblings.

We are taking Maddie to the courthouse tomorrow at four to give her a mock run of what the trial will be like. She asked if her friends would be there. I'd appreciate it if any of you can make it.

One by one, the replies came in and everyone was the same. They would all be there. He knew that he thought Hannah and Maddie were amazing, but he was glad to know that his family did too. He should have known that his family would know this meant something to him and therefore they would do their best to help if they could.

Chapter Seven

The following morning, Maddie was more subdued than usual, but the adults could understand that. When Deke arrived, Riley filled him in on the plan before he left to follow Hannah to work. Riley drove Maddie to school and just before she got out, he took her hand. "You have a good day at school Maddie and don't be nervous about this afternoon. Everybody is going to be there, and they are all going to be supporting you all the way. Okay?"

Maddie wrapped her arms around Riley's neck and said "Okay, Riley, I will try to be brave."

"Oh, Maddie you are so brave already, you don't know just how strong you are, and we are all so proud of you for doing this." Riley assured.

When she let go of him, he promised that he would be right there in the usual spot when school got over. He went around and helped her out of his big truck and stood there and watched until she was all the way into the school building before, he got in the truck and headed to the motorcycle shop. He had been sleeping fairly well the last few nights so he might as well go see if his brothers needed any help for a few hours.

"So, what's this thing you need us all at the courthouse for?" Bryan asked.

"Actually, Jeremy set it up. He got permission to use a room that will be empty. We'll show Maddie where everyone will sit. What the room looks like and all that. I appreciate that you said you'd be there. Is Sophie going to be able to make it?" Riley asked.

"Yep, she wouldn't miss it for the world. She thinks Hannah and Maddie are pretty great. She also seems to think that you and Hannah have something going on." Bryan said. There was no judgement in his tone, just curiosity.

"We've kissed a few times and yeah, we are hoping to go on a date, but we're keeping it away from Maddie until we know for sure how we feel about each other. I'm not going to jump into anything with her and she feels the same way. We'll get Maddie through this trial and maybe go on a date or two, but we have both agreed to be very careful. We don't want to give her anything more to process until we know if we even have anything that will last." Riley explained.

"Just be smart about it. That's all I ask." Bryan said. "No, you know what that was an asshole statement to make. I know you'll be smart about it. I just worry cause you're my little brother and I don't want to see you get hurt and I also don't want to see a little kid like Maddie get caught in the middle of more crap."

"I got it." Riley said. "I have a few hours to waste, any bikes you need me to work on?"

Bryan pointed out a bike and told him what needed to be done and he got to work.

****

Later that afternoon, Riley picked up Maddie from school and headed to the courthouse. Deke and Hannah shouldn't be far behind them. They waited outside until Hannah got there and then all went in to find Jeremy. He and Summer were waiting right near the door and a little further ahead were Bryan, Sophie, and Trevor.

"Look, Maddie," Hannah said "all of our new friends are here with us today.

Maddie just beamed a big smile at each of them. They all followed Jeremy to the room he had gotten for them.

"So" Jeremy began "This is where you will sit when it's your turn to talk" He showed Maddie to the witness stand. "Right up there is where the judge will sit. Do you have someone you want to pretend to be the judge for today?"

Maddie nodded "I want Sophie to be the judge." Sophie made her way to the judge's seat.

"Now, this chair right here," Jeremy said pulling out a chair at one of the tables, this is where the bad man will sit. Who do you want to pretend to be the bad man?"

Maddie just shook her head for a minute. "No one here can be the bad man; these are all my friends."

Jeremy thought for a moment, "Hang on let me check something." He pulled out his phone and set a text message to someone. A minute later he apparently got a reply. A few minutes later, one of the other owners of the brewery walked in the door. Pete was a familiar face to everyone except Hannah and Maddie because the Lawson brothers had worked on a body guarding job for him. In fact, that was how Bryan had met Sophie. Before he could say much Jeremy pulled him aside to explain quietly what was going on. He was hoping that having a stranger be the bad man might make it okay for Maddie. Everyone else must have understood what was going on because no one said much to Pete, not even Sophie and he was her brother.

"So, Maddie, I asked this man to come here and play the part of the bad man. He's not a bad man, but he's not one of your friends either. Is it okay for him to pretend to be the bad man?" Jeremy asked. Maddie nodded so Jeremy continued. "Great, so the bad man will be sitting right here in this chair." Pete took the appointed chair. And almost immediately, Riley and Deke took the two chairs immediately behind him. Hannah sat next to Riley. Bryan and Trevor sat beside Deke and Summer who took the seat next to Hannah. The whole front row was filled with her new friends.

"Now, if the judge asks you to point out who the bad man is, what will you do?" Jeremy asked.

Maddie looked up and timidly pointed toward Pete. But Pete had been told how this needed to go, so he gave her the best mean look he could. Riley saw her look of confidence fade a little. "You can do this Maddie, you don't have to look at the bad man, because look who's right behind him. I'm here, and Deke's here and you're mom's here. Do you think Deke and I or Bryan and Trevor for that matter would let the bad man do anything to you?" She slightly shook her head. So, Riley went a step further. "Would you mind standing up for a second, 'bad man'?"

Pete stood up and Riley stood right behind him. "Now, Maddie, if he was to try anything, do you think he could win in a fight with me?" She shook her head no a little more confidently. "Right, now" he looked over at Deke and Deke stood up. "If he was to try anything now, do you think he could win a fight with me and Deke together?" A smile lit her face, and she shook her head even more adamantly, Bryan and Trevor then stood forming a line of very solid and very intimidating muscle behind Pete.

"Now, Maddie" Jeremy asked, "Can you show me who the bad man is?"

Without any hesitation at all, Maddie pointed her finger directly at Pete and said, "Right there, that's the bad man!"

"Very good Maddie!" Riley said. "Now, Deke and I can't actually stand up behind him, we have to stay in our seats, but you get the idea, right? If the bad man tries anything at all, we will be right here to make sure you are safe."

Maddie's smile lit the whole room. They practiced a few more times with everyone sitting and each time that Maddie proclaimed Pete as the bad man, Sophie judged him guilty and told him he was going to go where he could never hurt any children ever again.

When they were done, Riley wanted to make sure one thing got cleared up in Maddie's mind. He went to Maddie and asked if he could pick her up for a minute. He had never really carried her anywhere before, but he had often lifted her out of his truck, and she had given him numerous hugs. She was fine with him carrying her, so he did. He thought that might be the best way to handle this next part. He walked toward where Pete was standing and motioned for Hannah to come too. When they were standing in front of Pete, Riley could feel Maddie's arm holding to him tightly. "Maddie, I want you to know that this is not a bad man. He is a friend of mine. His name is Pete, and actually, he's Sophie's brother." Sophie walked over and gave Pete a hug and thanked him for coming. "See, he's not a bad man, but we had to have someone you didn't know pretend to be a bad man for our practice."

"I promise he's not a bad man, Maddie. In fact, he's going to be having a little girl of his own any day now." Sophie assured.

"You're going to have a baby?" Maddie asked.

"Well, my wife Autumn is but yes, we're having a little girl of our own pretty soon. I actually love kids and would never hurt one." Pete assured. "I'm sorry I had to give you a mean face, but we wanted you to know that the real bad man may not be nice when he looks at you in court. He's going to try to scare you into not pointing him out as the bad man."

"Right, but like we showed you, he may try to be scary, but we won't let anything happen to you." Deke chimed in.

"Okay" Maddie said, her attention had already moved on to the new topic though "When Autumn has her baby can I come see it. I like babies. I have a cousin that was a baby, but now he's not a baby, he's bigger."

"I'm sure we can work that out." Sophie said. "Since Pete is my brother maybe you and I can go see the baby or maybe he will bring her to my house sometime when you come over."

"Yay!" Maddie exclaimed.

"I have a suggestion, if I may." Pete said. "I was planning to head over to the Pizzaria to meet Autumn for dinner, you are all welcome to tag along. I'm sure we can figure out seating. And, since I had to pretend to be the bad man, dinner is on me."

Riley looked to Hannah and just gave a shrug; it was completely up to her. She nodded so he agreed. "That sounds good Pete, we'll meet you there in a bit." He deposited Maddie back on the floor, but she grabbed onto his hand and took her mother's hand on the other side. They walked out of the courthouse hand in hand. They probably looked like a typical close knit family to anyone that would see them and that was just fine with Riley.

When they all arrived at the pizza place a short time later, Pete had indeed gotten a section of tables saved for all of them. Maddie was very excited to meet Autumn and she told her that Pete and Sophie said that they would let her meet the baby after it was born.

Chapter Eight

On Tuesday, they got the call that Maddie was supposed to come in on Wednesday and her statement would be recorded on video so that both attorney's had time to review it. She would then have to come to court on either Thursday or Friday to be able to identify the man. She only needed to be in the courtroom briefly, but it was always better if she could identify him in person in the courtroom because then there was no chance of mistaken identity. They did their best to prepare her for the situation and tried to keep her mind off of it as much as possible during the day.

Riley was finding that his sleep pattern was pretty much normal. He was sleeping at night, and he credited that to the fact that every night after Maddie went to bed, he and Hannah spent some time talking and kissing on the couch. Every night she wished him sweet dreams before she went down the hall to go to bed.

Maddie gave her testimony on video coming across as a very strong little girl. She had met the prosecutor before and was comfortable with talking to him. She was a little shy when she talked about some of the things that had happened, mostly because in her mind those were adult things that she wasn't comfortable talking about. Hannah was allowed to be in the room, behind the camera tripod as long as she kept quiet and didn't influence Maddie's statement in any way.

Riley paced the hallway outside of the conference room, He was worried about how both of his girls were going to handle this. He knew it wouldn't be easy for Maddie to talk about, but it also wouldn't be easy for Hannah to hear. She already knew the facts, but to hear her daughter have to talk about it and answer questions wasn't going to be easy. When they walked out of the room, Riley couldn't help himself, he picked Maddie up in one arm and wrapped Hannah in the other and held them both close to him hoping that he could offer them both some strength. He realized it was the first time Maddie had seen any sigh of physical connection between him and Hannah but if she had any questions, he could easily explain it by saying that he thought they could both use a hug after what couldn't have been a fun experience for both of them. He wasn't saying much other than "It's okay, that part's over now." Simple statements made to hopefully soothe both of them.

"I think we're going to be okay, right Maddie?" Hannah said.

"Um hmm." was all Maddie added.

Riley took that as a sign that he should probably let Hannah go, he wasn't sure he wanted to let Maddie go. "You okay with me carrying you out to the truck?" he asked. "I just need to hug you a little longer."

"Yes Riley." Maddie said "I would like that. You make me feel safe."

That was the best compliment he had ever been given and if holding her made her feel safe he would hold her every minute that he could. "I was thinking maybe we should get our favorite pizza tonight and if mom doesn't mind maybe we can have a scoop of ice cream too." he offered.

"That sounds good to me." Hannah said.

They stopped for pizza and ice cream on the way home. When they got there, Maddie asked if they could watch Moana again. Riley was all for whatever made her feel good. It had been a very difficult day for all of them. This time though, Maddie sat on his lap for the entire movie and by the time it was over, she was pretty much asleep. Riley carried her down to her bedroom and tucked her into bed. Both adults gave her a kiss goodnight and wished her sweet dreams.

When they got back to the living room, Riley asked the question he had been dying to ask all evening. "How did it go?"

"Well, Maddie took it like a real trooper. I could tell she wasn't comfortable talking about it, but she didn't shy away from telling them the truth. She was a lot stronger than I think I would have been if it had been me." Hannah stated. "I think a lot of that is due to you and Deke and all of your family and friends. Maddie has always had family, but now she has a whole new family standing behind her and it makes her strong. Thank you for being there for both of us Riley."

He held his arms open, and she stepped into him. "I wouldn't want to be anywhere else Hannah. You and Maddie are becoming more and more important to me. When this is all over, we will have some time to just be us and see where we want things to go. In the meantime, I'm here for you and Maddie in any way that I can be." He kissed the top of her head and she just stood there in his arms for a long time.

Finally, she pulled away and said, "I think I'm going to head to bed, it's been a long day and I have a feeling I won't feel better about things until this is over." She stood up on her tip toes and kissed Riley on the cheek. "Good night Riley, sweet dreams."

Riley had too much pent up energy to be able to sleep, so he made sure that the front door was locked and went out into the backyard. He did sit ups then push ups until his body couldn't do anymore and then he went back inside. He found Hannah sitting on the couch. "Hey sweetheart, is something wrong?"

"No, I just couldn't sleep, so I came out here to talk to you. I thought you had left but I looked out front and your truck is still there, so I looked out back and saw you. I didn't want to interrupt so I just sat here and waited." she sounded small and maybe a little scared.

Riley walked over and scooped her up in his arms and then sat back on the couch with her in his lap. "There are so many things wrong with that statement" he began. "First, I wouldn't leave unless I had to and if I had to, I would make sure someone else was here before I did. I won't leave the two of you alone. Second you could have come outside and found me. I was just burning off some steam. You don't ever have to just sit and wait. I'm here for you whenever you need me, Hannah." He was gently stroking her back as he spoke.

"Okay." Hannah said softly. "I just couldn't sleep" She laid her head on Riley's chest and just listened to his heartbeat. It wasn't long before she drifted off to sleep in his arms. Riley didn't want to disturb her if this was the only way she could sleep, he would deal with it. He shifted slightly so that he could rest his head on the back of the sofa and held her closely. It was several hours later when she woke up. "Oh, I'm sorry." she said as she woke up.

"Nothing to apologize for." Riley stated, "I actually drifted off too."

"But what if Maddie…" she began.

Riley placed a finger over her lips. "First, Maddie didn't wake up so that's nothing to be concerned about. Second, if she had woke up, I don't think she would be upset by it. She knows you had a hard day too and maybe you just needed a hug. We fell asleep, no big deal. I think you are so worried about Maddie that you are letting yourself stress over every little thing. I get that she's your daughter and you want to protect her, but I don't think she would have a problem with it even if she did figure out, we liked each other."

"I know." Hannah agreed. "She loves you already, I just don't want her confused until you and I figure out what we have."

"I get that but falling asleep in my arms isn't a big deal. I think she would understand that you just needed a hug and we ended up falling asleep." Riley assured.

"Yeah, you're probably right." Hannah said. "I should go to bed though so that you can get more comfortable." Riley let her go but before she walked down the hall she softly said, "thank you Riley."

"Anytime sweetheart."

They both slept for a few more hours before Hannah came walking out of her bedroom with a strange look on her face. She held her phone in her hands. "That was the prosecutor, Maddie needs to be in court at ten Friday morning." She didn't say any more, they both knew what that meant.

Riley picked up his phone and started making calls. He called one of the leaders of BACA so that they could rally whoever could be there and then he called Bryan. As the oldest, he would make sure Riley's siblings knew. He asked Bryan to make sure that Summer passed the word on to Jeremy too. He wasn't sure how many of them could be there. Everyone had jobs, but he wanted them all to know so that they could be there in spirit if nothing else. Hannah had opted to not tell Maddie until Thursday night because she didn't want it affecting her daughter's school days.

On Thursday night, after dinner, the four of them sat at the table and talked about the next day. Deke usually didn't stay for dinner, but tonight he wanted to be there. They made the plan for how the following morning would go and then Deke headed home to rest for the next day.

Maddie asked "Mommy, can I sleep with you tonight?" Of course, her mother said yes. "Can Riley sleep with us too?"

Hannah looked at Riley and he gave a slight shrug to let her know it was completely up to her. "Sure, Maddie, that's fine."

When they went to bed, Maddie was tucked safely between them. "Thank you for being here for us, Riley." she said.

"You're welcome, Maddie. There's no place else I'd rather be."

Maddie gave them each a kiss and said good night.

"Good night Maddie, good night Riley, sweet dreams for both of you." Hannah said. She truly hoped her daughter could have sweet dreams.

A couple of times during the night, Maddie started to thrash a little like she was having a nightmare, but Riley just put a calming hand on her shoulder and Hannah kissed her on the forehead and she settled back down. Both of the adults would be so happy when this was over. For Maddie it would feel over after today. They both knew it wouldn't fully be over until he was found guilty, sentenced, and hopefully going to prison for a long time.

Chapter Nine

The following morning, they walked out of the house at a quarter after nine. Riley had thought he had heard motorcycles a few minutes before, but he assumed it was Deke and maybe his brothers. What he hadn't been sure he would see was the line of at least thirty motorcycles lined up along the side of the road. He knew at least a few of the members would be there, but it was never a guarantee how many could make it on a workday. Especially when they weren't sure how many would be allowed into the courthouse. When they got to the side of Riley's truck, he pulled out the small vest that had been given to Maddie that first day they met. As loudly as he could, he said. "Blaze today all of your friends are here to go with you to court. We will stand beside you and support you every step of the way." Everyone in the yard and along the road gave a loud cheer and Riley continued "Blaze, are you ready to ride?" When Maddie said yes, he helped her into her vest and then into his truck. He backed out of the driveway and hesitated a minute until everyone had the time to get their bikes started and in line. He looked in the rear view mirror and then lifted his head to indicate that Hannah should look behind them.

When she turned, Hanna couldn't believe her eyes at just how long of a line they had behind them. "Look Maddie, turn around and see just how many people are here to help you be strong."

Maddie turned and her eyes got as big as saucers and a large smile came over her face.

"We can do this, can't we Blaze?" Riley asked.

"Yes, we can." Maddie said with triumph.

When they arrived at the courthouse, they were just walking up the steps with their entire entourage following behind them when they heard a voice say, "Why hello, Maddie." They turned to see the man that Maddie was here to testify against. Standing there with a big smile on his face. It was barely seconds before Riley, Bryan and Trevor formed a human wall in front of Maddie and the man was in a chokehold with Deke's strong arm around his neck. Maddie had noticeably flinched at the sound of his voice but stood strong when she realized that she had a human shield in front of her.

Riley and his brothers then turned, and Riley said, "Let's go inside." As they all began walking with Maddie and Hannah in the front and the Lawson brothers a solid wall behind them, Riley said over his shoulder "Some of you guys wanna make sure Deke doesn't kill him, we don't need to have to visit him in jail."

"Oh, I'm not going to kill him," Deke said "although I want to. But I will make sure he stays right here until you guys are inside." The man was sweating profusely and looked like he was about ready to pee his own pants.

The group continued inside where they found Jeremy standing waiting for them "Hey, I just wanted to let you guys know that there's been a change in what courtroom you're going to. At their puzzled look he continued "Well, I had a talk with the judge, and he realized that we would need a bigger room so that as many of Maddie's friends as possible could be in the room. I don't think everyone will fit even with the change but, it's better than it was."

"Thank you, I don't know what strings you pulled but thank you." Riley said.

"Some days it pays to be the son of a Senator."

Several minutes later, they were seated in the front row of the courtroom on the defendant's side. However, a few minutes later, a bailiff came out and asked Hannah and Maddie to come with him. Riley asked what was going on and the bailiff wouldn't say much but he did let Riley follow them to the front area of the courthouse. "The judge was told that the defendant approached you on the courtroom steps and spoke to the victim." he addressed his question to Hannah, "Is this correct?"

"It is" Hannah said simply.

"The judge would like you and your daughter to be sequestered until it's time for her testimony. You and she can wait in a side room there is a closed circuit TV in there but it's up to you if you want to watch it or not."

"Okay" Hannah agreed.

"I would suggest that you go back and take your seat, Sir. There will be no way to get you back in the seat in time when the victim takes the stand, and I am sure that you want to be seated where you were when the defendant comes into the room." he suggested.

"But how did he…" Hannah began looking around. Riley was looking too and when he spotted Walt, he directed Hannah's attention to him. Walt just winked and gave a short nod and then walked back out of the room. Apparently, he had seen what had happened and had found the judge in his chambers

Riley leaned down and told Maddie "You go with your mom; I'll be sitting right where we practiced." He gave her a one arm squeeze hug and then made his way back to his seat. A short time later, the defendant walked into the room with his attorney and noticeably flinched when he saw Deke sitting right behind him.

When the judge took the stand his first words were "It has been brought to my attention that the defendant approached the victim on the steps of the courthouse, therefore violating the restraining order and terms of his bail. Regardless of how long this trial takes up to and including sentencing if the verdict comes out as guilty, the defendant is remanded to custody, bail is revoked."

A murmur of approval went across the courtroom, but the defendant began to argue. The judge looked him right in the eye and said "I would suggest that you remain quiet until your attorney tells you to speak. I do not look highly on defendants that take actions such as yours today and if you so much as utter a sound, I will add contempt of court to your charges. Do I make myself clear?"

The defendant simply nodded.

Riley wanted to chuckle at the predicament the man found himself in, but he was glad for a judge that didn't take things like that lightly and for friends that helped take care of his Maddie. And she was, she was totally his Maddie, just like Hannah was his Hannah. Oh, they had logistics to work out, but they were going to be his for the rest of their lives.

When it came time for Maddie to take the stand, the bailiff went and got both Maddie and Hannah, he let Hannah be the one to help her little girl into the chair. From there it was a pretty simple procedure. The judge simply said, Maddie, I have seen the tape of the statement you made a few days ago and your answers to the questions. I don't need to know anything more about what you say happened to you. The only thing I need to know is whether or not the man who did those things is in this room and if he is can you point him out?"

Maddie nodded and then looked up. She looked right straight at the defendant and then behind him at the room full of people who were there to support her. Every single one of those faces was encouraging her to be strong, so she was. She pointed and said "That's the bad man right there. That's the man who I was talking about on the tape."

The defense attorney started to say "I object" but that was all he got out before the judge shut him down.

"Look counselor, if you think for one minute, I'm going to allow you to grandstand in front of this child, you would be wrong. She has positively identified him as the bad man, and even if I did question the validity of that statement, and I don't, your client made himself look guilty by trying to approach her outside." the judge warned. "I would assume that there are people in this courtroom that would be willing to testify to the fact that he violated the restraining order. Would I be right?" He looked out over the room and every single hand was raised. "Just as I thought. Without any further delay, I find the defendant guilty of all of the charges against him and I bind him over for sentencing to be conducted two weeks from today. Bailiff if you would escort the defendant to the county jail, I am sure they have a nice jumpsuit and a nice cell for him to sit in while he waits."

"Your Honor, my client was assaulted on his way into the courthouse today by this band of hooligans." the attorney said pointing behind him.

"I had a feeling you would go there, so I made sure to watch the security camera feed before coming in here. What I saw was a man who is a member of an organization that I respect restraining a criminal who was attempting to make contact with his victim. An act that was strictly forbidden by this court in a previous order. Would you like to continue to try to make excuses for your client?" the judge asked.

The attorney finally realize that he was far better off keeping his mouth shut. "No, Your Honor."

"Good, bailiff please escort the defendant out of here." When the bailiff had taken the man out of the room, the judge turned to Maddie "Young lady, I would like to thank you for being here today and helping me take a bad man off of the streets. You and your friends here are heroes in my opinion. Don't ever think that you have to let bad people hurt you. You tell your mom, you tell your friends out there, or you tell a police officer because we can't help you make bad people go away if we don't know they are doing bad things."

Maddie just smiled at him and nodded.

"And on that note, I would like to thank all of you for what you do for the kids that don't often get a voice." He scanned the room and nodded to the members of BACA then he said, "and with that, court is adjourned."

He stood and left the courtroom and Maddie and Hannah met Riley halfway when he approached them. He wrapped them both in a hug. When he pulled back, he looked down at Maddie and said you don't have to worry about seeing him for a long time."

"How long?" Maddie asked.

"Well, the judge has to decide that in two weeks, but until then, he's in jail so he can't come and hurt you." Hannah said.

"Does that mean that Riley and Deke won't come stay with us anymore?" Maddie asked.

By this time, Deke had made his way to them too. "Nope, we're here for a little while longer, Maddie."

"And like I told you even when I'm not assigned to you with BACA, you and I will still be friends." Riley encouraged.

"Okay." Maddie said.

"Hey Maddie would you want to go talk to Sophie; I have to talk to your mom for a minute." Riley had not missed the look of surprise on Hannah's face when Deke said they were sticking around, but he didn't want to say anything in front of Maddie. When Maddie was busy telling Sophie how happy she was that the bad man was going away.

"Hannah, I saw the look when Deke said we're staying around. Technically, yes, BACA sticks close until the guy has gone to prison, and even then, we check back in. But I'm not going anywhere anytime soon. There is something between us and I want to see where it's going. I'm here for as long as you'll have me." Riley said.

Hannah just smiled. When they turned to walk out of the room, Maddie ran up to them "Mommy, Sophie wants to know if I can come over for a sleepover tomorrow or the next day."

"Well, maybe tomorrow, since it's Saturday." Hannah said. She looked to Sophie and asked, "Are you sure it's, okay?"

"Totally okay, Sempre Fi has been hoping Maddie would come and play with her again sometime soon." Sophie assured. "You guys can come for lunch if you want and then head out so Maddie and I can have some girl time."

"Okay, if, you're sure." Hannah said.

"Yay!" Maddie exclaimed. They walked out of the building hand in hand again. Riley was liking how this already felt like family to him.

Chapter Ten

The following morning Maddie asked about every ten minutes if it was time to go yet. Each time she asked, Hannah sent her to check to make sure she had packed a different item so that Maddie would go check her bag for the item. Finally at about eleven o'clock, Riley took pity on both of them and announced it was time to go for lunch. It was actually a little early, but he was sure Bryan and Sophie wouldn't mind. He sent a quick text to let them know that they were on their way and why and then they headed out the door.

When they arrived, Maddie ran to the door as soon as she was free of the truck, but Hannah cautioned "Maddie, use your manners and wait for us or you won't be staying."

"Yes Mommy." She tried to patiently wait on the porch for the adults to catch up. Before they had though, the door opened. "I didn't knock, how did you know I was here?" she asked Sophie.

"Oh, trust me, when you have Trevor in your family, there are all kinds of security cameras and hi-tech gadgets to let you know when someone is here." Sophie assured.

Maddie looked confused at that statement but by that time Semper Fi had come out the door and the little girl had all the distraction she needed.

"I'm sorry we're so early." Hannah apologized. "Maddie was asking every ten minutes if it was time to leave yet, so Riley made the decision to come over now."

"It's no problem." Sophie assured. "If you want you can come help me, put the lunch together and Riley and Maddie can head out back. Bryan's out there."

They made their way to the kitchen and had a pleasant chat while they put together a simple lunch of sandwiches and chips with a fruit tray. Riley and Maddie took the puppy and went to the back yard. Maddie was busy playing tag with the puppy, so Bryan took the opportunity to talk to Riley. "You guys are going out tonight then?"

"Planning on it. Look, Bryan, I'm not jumping into anything with her. We've been spending a lot of time talking and getting to know each other. I've been living there for weeks." Riley defended.

"I know." Bryan admitted. "And I don't really have a problem with that, I guess it's just that this situation is complicated. She's your client in one sense."

Riley scoffed at Bryan "Pot meet kettle. Sophie was your client when you hooked up with her."

"I know, and that's why I'm telling you to be careful. I'm not telling you not to do it, I'm just saying that there's a lot involved here, including a little girl. You can't screw this up. Not that I think you would intend to, but just be careful, okay?"

"I am, that's why we haven't really done much more than talk and kiss a little when Maddie was asleep." Riley explained. "Tonight, I hope that we can be more free to see where things are."

"Okay." Bryan agreed "And if it makes any difference, I hope it works out for you. Hannah and Maddie seem like really great people."

"They definitely are." Riley wasn't going to tell his brother that he had already pretty much decided that they were going to be his one way or another. His brother might argue that it was too soon to know that, but it wasn't. Riley had been with them practically twenty-four seven for weeks. He knew what he was getting into.

The lunch was relaxing and enjoyable, but Riley was so ready to leave. He wanted time with Hannah, time to just do whatever they wanted and not have to worry about it confusing Maddie as to what was going on with her mommy and her friend. Apparently, Hannah must have felt the same way because soon after they were finished eating, she asked Maddie "Are you sure you're going to be okay spending the night?"

"Yes, Mommy. I have Sophie and Bryan to take care of me and Sempre Fi too." Maddie stated. "Are you going to miss me mommy?"

"I will miss you, but I will be okay as long as I know you are okay." Hannah said.

"Yay!" Maddie exclaimed.

Riley decided there was no time like the present to ask, "Are you ready to go then Hannah?"

"Sure, I'm ready, let's get out of here so that Maddie can have fun." Hannah stated.

They both headed out and Bryan walked them to the front porch. "You know I was just being a big brother earlier, right?" he asked Riley.

"I know." Riley said. He leaned in and gave his brother a handshake and one arm hug and then they left.

"What was that about with Bryan?" Hannah asked.

"Oh, he just told me the usual big brother stuff, to be careful because of Maddie and because technically, you're still the client as far as BACA is concerned." Riley explained.

"Oh." was all Hannah could say.

"Look, like I told you, it's not a problem with BACA and we're being careful with Maddie, that's why she's there. Bryan has no room to talk anyway since Sophie was a bodyguard job for him and he slept with her basically the whole time he was guarding her." Riley explained. "He's just doing what he's always done and trying to watch out for all of us."

"Okay, and I appreciate that you were okay with making this secret for now until we know where we stand so that it doesn't confuse Maddy."

"That's no problem sweetheart, but I already know where I stand. I want you and Maddie both in my life for the foreseeable future." Riley said. "Now, what would you like to do with our day?"

"Well, I'd like to find out who you are. I feel like you know so many things about me and I don't know much about you. I know you've told me about the bike shop and your house, but I want to see what you want to show me."

"Sweetheart, you know things that no one knows about me from my time in Iraq, but I'd be glad to show you more of me." Riley stated. He headed for the motorcycle shop. When he parked his truck, he noticed that summer's shop was open too. Might as well include the full tour. He showed her to the tattoo parlor first. When they walked in the bell over the door announced their arrival. Summer came out of the back room.

"Hey little brother." she greeted stepping up to him to offer a hug. "Hi Hannah. What are you two doing here?"

"Well, Hannah wanted to know more about who I am, so I'm showing her the shop and all that. I noticed you were open so I thought we would stop in and say hi." Riley explained.

"Welcome." Summer said to Hannah. "It's pretty much what it looks like a basic tattoo shop. If you ever decide you want any ink let me know, but if you don't that's totally cool too. They aren't for everyone."

"I'm sure it's a fascinating process. And I definitely think you have huge talent. The work I have seen has been great." Hannah praised.

"Thank you." Summer said. "Where's Maddie today?"

"She's having a sleep over at Bryan and Sophie's" Riley stated. "We wanted a chance to get out and maybe get to know each other a little without giving Maddie the wrong impression."

"That's cool, I hope you have a fun day." Summer said.

They talked for a few more minutes and then headed next door. Riley showed her the garage part of the business as well as the store where they sold clothing and motorcycle accessories. "There's an apartment upstairs too, I won't show it to you because it's pretty much just a place we crash when we work late so I never know if it's going to be clean or not. Although, right now, the only one that probably uses it would be Trevor. Bryan goes home every night, and I've been staying with you. So, it might not be too bad."

"It's quite a business. I had no idea you guys were so successful." Hannah said. She was impressed. The shop was large, they could fit several motorcycles in there at one time and a few were in the various bays. The shop was no small thing. It would rival most stores of its nature; they had a large area, and it was filled with Harley gear as well as helmets and accessories.

"Well, Bryan started it up shortly after he got home from the Marines. Pops helped him get it going. It was just a small shop a few blocks from here at that time. Over the years as Trevor and I joined him, we were able to expand it and buy this building. When the space became available, we added the store and then a few years ago, the building next door went up and we offered to help Summer buy it. She's pretty sure we only offered so that Bryan and Trevor could keep an eye on her and she's probably right to some extent. They like knowing that she's close by in case she has any trouble."

"Impressive." That was the only word Hannah could think to say. These siblings who had lost their parents at a young age had banded together to make a business they should be proud of.

"Well, it's mostly Bryan and Trevor." Riley said.

"Bullshit" a voice said from somewhere above them. Riley and Hannah looked up to see Trevor coming down the stairs from the apartment above. "We all did this. Yeah, Bryan and I started it because you were still enlisted, but since you've gotten back, you've been an asset to both businesses."

"Right, you said you guys do some bodyguard and private investigative stuff too right. That's how you all met Sophie." Hannah said.

"That's how we met all of the Five Sloth guys. Pete hired us." Riley said.

"Yeah, don't let Riley try to fool you. He's got the spidey sense that has saved our asses on more than one occasion. We don't know how he does it sometimes, but he sees and hears things no one else does and it's spot on every time." Trevor said.

"Well, we all have our strengths" Riley said humbly. "None of us can run tech like you do."

"Sounds like you make a great team then." Hannah said.

"Yeah, we do." Trevor said. "Well, I just finished up the bike I was working on and went upstairs to clean up. I'm headed out soon. What are you two up to?"

"Hannah wanted to know more about who I am and what I do so I'm showing her around. It's our first date of sorts." Riley said.

"Awesome, have fun." Trevor said as he walked over to close his tool chest. That was Trevor, the laid back one, oh, he could be just as deadly as the rest of them, but for the most part, he would harm you by hacking into your bank account and making it look like you were doing illegal things. Trevor seemed mellow, but that was because he was all stealth. He could be in and out of an operation without ever leaving a trace.

"Well, you ready to head out, sweetheart?" Riley asked.

"Sure." Hannah agreed.

"I was thinking if you would like, I'd stop at the store and pick up some stuff to cook dinner for you tonight at my place. I'm not a great cook, but I have a few dishes that I do well. You've fed me a lot of meals the least I can do is return the favor." Riley said.

"That sounds good." Hannah agreed.

Chapter Eleven

They stopped at a grocery store and Riley picked up the ingredients to make her a nice dinner then drove to his house. His home wasn't as large or as fancy as Bryan's, but it was still bigger than Hannah's house. It was a three bedroom farmhouse. "It's not huge, but I like living here. We grew up in the country and none of us except Summer live in a place where you can see your neighbors."

"It's beautiful" Hannah said. "I can see where your line of lilacs are, they must be so beautiful in the Spring."

"It's early for dinner. Do you want to go sit in the backyard and talk or do you want to watch a movie? It's up to you sweetheart." he encouraged.

"We can sit outside, it's a beautiful day." Hannah said.

"Do you want something to drink before we go out?" Riley asked.

"Sure, I'll take whatever." she replied.

"I've got wine, beer, water and pop." Riley said.

Hannah was a little surprised because most men didn't keep wine on hand, although Riley probably invited women over often enough that he kept some on hand. "I'll take wine then."

"I know absolutely nothing about wine. Summer insists that I keep a few bottles here for when she comes over. I do know that I have red, and I have white. That's the extent of what I know about wine.' He pulled a bottle out of the cupboard and one out of the fridge.

"Apparently you also know that red is served at room temperature and white is served chilled." Hannah said with a smile.

"Yeah, I was keeping it all in the cupboard until I offered Summer a glass and she was ticked that the white was warm." Riley chuckled.

"I'll take the white." Hannah said.

Riley poured her a glass and then grabbed a beer for himself. He showed her out onto his back deck.

This was a backyard a little girl like Maddie would dream of having Hannah thought. It was large and there was a pool. It wasn't a huge one, but it was a pool. There was room for a lot of things that she didn't have room for like a trampoline and one of those wooden structures that could have a swing and slides and a fort. Hannah had a simple swing set that was really all she had room for. "It's a great backyard."

"Thanks." Riley said. "If you think you and Maddie would like to swim sometime just let me know."

"I'm sure she would love it." Hannah said.

They sat on a bench that overlooked the lawn and the woods at the back of the property. They were quiet just enjoying their beverages and the beautiful day. Riley got Hannah's attention and pointed to the edge of the woods. There was a mother deer and her fawn munching on the corn that Riley left out for the animals that visited him.

"That's so cool." Hannah said softly so as not to disturb them. "I've never lived in the country, so this is cool for me."

"I put out corn and sometimes other things to attract them. I've never been one that wanted to hunt so I like to have them come to my yard so I can enjoy them."

"It's beautiful out here." she said with a smile.

After they sat for a while and just enjoyed the wildlife and the sunshine, Riley said "Look, Hannah. It's kind of weird I guess; this is our first date, but I feel like I know you so well already. We've talked and kissed and spent so much time together that this doesn't feel like a first date to me. It just feels like we are spending time together alone. But I know that the one aspect of this that is a concern for you is having Maddie get confused. I respect that as a mother you don't want to see her get hurt. But I don't plan to go anywhere anytime soon. And I definitely don't plan to hurt Maddie. I'm willing to play this however you want to play it with Maddie, but I think she would be okay with the idea of us dating."

Hannah thought about that for a while. "I'm sure you're probably right. She would definitely love the idea of you being around for a long time. I am just so protective of her now. I know that what happened to her is my fault. I should have protected her; I should have known there was something going on." Tears were silently rolling down her face.

Riley scooped her up and sat her in his lap. "That is absolutely not true, Hannah. You can't protect a child every minute of every day. These people know exactly how to make you feel comfortable with them. They know how to make parents and kids feel safe. They are always the typical nice guy next door or the sweet lady down the street. No one would have any way of knowing that they are predators. Unless you want to lock them away and never let them walk down the street or go to a friend's house, no one can be absolutely certain that nothing will happen to them. All you can do is what you have already done. You've stood beside her; you've supported her and honestly sweetheart a huge part of what you have done is believed her. So many parents don't. Either they just don't want to face it, or they don't want to think that nice Mr. Jones down the street could be that way. Especially when it's a family member or a close family friend. Many parents don't listen to the kid and do way more harm. You didn't know but as soon as you did, you stood up for your daughter. She will never forget that. She will get past the things that he did, she's seeing her counselor and she has you and me and a whole support system if she needs it. But she will never forget who believed her and who stood behind her." He just held her and let his words sink in.

Several long minutes later she pulled her head from his chest and looked into his eyes. "You're a pretty awesome man, do you know that, Riley Lawson?"

"I'm not really all that special, but I'm glad you think so Hannah." He leaned in for a kiss and she happily complied. Their kisses turned more and more heated, and Hannah turned her body so that she could straddle Riley. Finally, Riley had the presence of mind to realize that they were getting way too carried away for what he wanted on a bench in his backyard. He pulled his face away slightly but put his forehead to hers and said "Hannah, I'd love to continue this in my bedroom. If you don't want that, it's fine, But I can't keep doing this out here, my house is fairly secluded, but you never know for sure."

"I'd like that, Riley." she said softly.

Riley didn't need any more consent than that to at least take her into his bedroom. He stood up and carried her inside and up the stairs. He deposited her on his bed and laid beside her. "We don't have to go any further than you want to sweetheart. If you want to stop, just say so." At her nod of acquiescence, he leaned in and began kissing her again.

Riley put his hand under her shirt to caress her stomach. She had the softest skin. He worked the bottom of the shirt up higher so that he had access to her softness. He had never seen her naked, but he was positive that she was going to be beautiful. She already was beautiful, but naked she would be beyond beautiful. He started to lift her shirt up so that he could remove it, but she stopped his hand. "Riley, I don't look all gorgeous and sexy. I have stretch marks and I have more weight than I should."

"Sweetheart, you have a child, I've never been with a woman that has a child before, not that I've been with many women at all, but I know that when a woman carries a child her body is never exactly the same. It's one of the miracles of life. It's kind of like how I look at my back. For a long time, I was worried about how ugly it was, but then my brother told me that I shouldn't be that way. It's a scar, well, lots of scars that show that I went through something that was hard and painful, but I came out on the other side of it, and I have the scars to show that I was strong enough to get through it. Stretch marks are the same thing. It's proof that you carried a child, you gave life to another human being. That's an amazing thing, Hannah. I'm not worried about a few stretch marks or a few pounds that you think you need to lose. I think you're beautiful and I would love the opportunity to worship and adore your body. But if you aren't ready, I can wait."

Hannah loved how beautiful Riley made her feel even with just words. "No, I want to continue, it's just that I haven't been with anyone since my husband died and I'm not in the shape I was before. But I do believe that you find me beautiful, and I want this with you."

Riley lifted Hannah's shirt and she raised up off the bed enough that he could pull it over her head. She had a pretty pink lacy bra on that was soft and feminine and sexy as hell as far as Riley was concerned. "I was right, you're absolutely beautiful." He leaned in and began kissing her stomach while his hands softly caressed her breasts through her bra. Yes, he saw a few stretch marks. He was sure there would be more on her lower abdomen too. No, she didn't have a flat stomach. He absolutely did not care, she was beautiful. He had told her he wanted to worship her body and that was exactly what he intended to do. He laid gentle kisses all over every inch of exposed flesh before he drew her bra straps off her shoulders. She again lifted so that he could remove it. He began kissing and licking her breast and nipples. Gently at first, he could hear the change in her breathing. She was definitely enjoying this. He took her nipple in his mouth and began sucking it and swirling his tongue around the tight flesh. Worshiping her body was all well and good, but he needed to kiss her too. He pulled his mouth away from her body and devoured her lips. His hand kept caressing her periodically rolling her nipple between his thumb and finger. He wanted to know just what gave her the most pleasure, so he began adding more and more pressure to her nipple with each pinch until she was moaning low in her throat. He noted the point that it had seemed to get the most response. He was going to learn all of the sweet spots and what got her the most aroused. He would spend the rest of tonight learning her and yes, there was a thought in his head that told him he would like to spend the rest of his life using all that he learned to pleasure her. Some might say it was way too early in the relationship for him to be thinking about forever, but he would disagree. His belief was that there was one person for everyone and when you knew you had found them, you just knew. Not that he would ever say that her husband dying was a good thing, but it was part of how the universe had brought him and his 'one' together. He hadn't dated a lot of women in his life because it never took him long to realize that there just wasn't a connection. His instincts had always told him that there was someone out there and when he found her, he would know. Now he was sure he had been right.

Riley needed to see the rest of her, so he unfastened her jeans. As he lowered the zipper, he saw that she had lacy pink panties on that matched her bra. He was pretty sure she had done that intentionally so that she would be pretty to him. What she didn't realize was that she could totally have been wearing the simplest of under garments and she would have been the most beautiful woman he had ever seen. He pulled her jeans down and she lifted off of the bed to make that possible. When he had her naked except for her panties, he just took a moment to look. "You are absolutely beautiful Hannah. More than I ever imagined." Yes, there were even more stretch marks just above the waistband of her underwear, they were beautiful too. What he had told her had been his honest belief. They were a testament to the fact that she was a mother, she had gone through the work of carrying another life inside her. That made her even more beautiful. For a brief moment, Riley could picture her belly round with child, his child. No, not anytime soon. He wasn't in any hurry to have any more of a family than he and Hannah and Maddie would be. But eventually, he would love to have a child with Hannah. He began his kissing again; he wanted every inch of her to feel loved and beautiful.

Hannah was pretty sure she was going to explode if Riley didn't move forward with this, His touching and kissing was amazing, but it was making it so that she needed more. It had been a long time since she had sex and she had never had anyone worship her like this before. "Please, Riley"

"Please what, Sweetheart?" he asked.

"I need more."

Riley slid her panties down and his lips were immediately on her pussy. He needed to taste her, and he wanted to give her all the pleasure he possibly could. He wanted her to orgasm before he entered her because he was pretty sure he wouldn't last long. It had been a while for him and with all of the kissing and touching they had been doing in the evenings, his body was more than ready. He needed her to be more than ready before he let himself off the leash. He licked and sucked at her clit until she was pressing herself against him to try to get more. He inserted two fingers inside her and began moving them in and out as he sucked her clit. The more she moved against him, the faster his fingers moved and the more pressure he put on her clit. She was thrashing so much that Riley almost had to fight to continue. It was only moments before she screamed her release. Riley could feel her muscles tighten on his hand and immediately he thought about how that would feel on his dick. He stopped sucking and stopped moving his fingers, but he kept himself firmly pressed against her. His warm mouth covering her clit and his fingers deep inside her. Finally, after the spasms had stopped, he stood and removed his clothing. He grabbed a condom from his nightstand and put it on quickly. He had lost all ability to wait any longer, but he would if she wasn't ready. He lay beside her on the bed and kissed her before he said "I want to be inside you so much, Hannah. Can I make love to you?"

"Yes, please Riley, I need it" Hannah replied.

That was all he needed to know. He moved over top of her and slowly moved his cock into her. He knew it had been a long time for her since she had sex and even though he had given her an orgasm, he didn't want to just shove into her and take any chance of causing her any pain. He wanted this entire experience to be nothing but pleasure for her.

When he was as deep as he could possibly go, he paused briefly to allow both of them a moment to just feel the sensations. That didn't last long because he needed to move inside her and she was trying to force movement from below him. He slowly withdrew and entered increasing his pace slightly after a few thrusts. He alternated between leaning down and kissing her deeply and pulling away to see the look on her beautiful face. "God Hannah, I just keep thinking how beautiful you are." he said.

She was meeting him with every thrust. Finally, they were both moving fast and hard against each other and soon he felt her tightening on him with the spasms of her orgasm. He couldn't hold out any longer, he thrust deeply into her and let himself go. He laid there for a minute before realizing that he was probably crushing her with his body weight. He didn't want to lose the connection of their bodies being so close, so he held her tightly as he rolled to the side. She stayed pressed up against him and softly said "Thank you, Riley."

"You don't have to thank me for making love to you, sweetheart. I got just as much pleasure from it as you did." he assured.

"I know but thank you for making me feel beautiful and worshiped." She sounded like she was going to drift off to sleep and that was fine with Riley. He would lay here and hold her for a bit before he needed to get up and go make their dinner. She did drift off to sleep, so he quietly extricated himself from her arms and went to grab a pair of shorts from his dresser. He laid a t-shirt of his on the bench at the end of the bed so that she could put it on if she wanted to. There wasn't much point in getting dressed if they were going to end up spending the night here in his house. Although he would take her home after dinner if that was what she preferred. Just because he wanted to spend the night with her didn't mean she wanted to spend the night with him.

Chapter Twelve

Forty-five minutes later, Hannah came padding down the stairs wearing Riley's t-shirt and nothing else. She hadn't wanted to put her underwear back on because they had gotten very wet from all of Riley's attention earlier. "Something smells amazing." she said as she walked into the kitchen.

Riley turned to see her, and he couldn't help himself, he sat down what he was doing and walked over to her. He wrapped an arm around her and drew her to him. "Thank you, sweetheart. I'm glad you found my shirt; I was hoping you would feel free to wear it." There was something about seeing his woman in his shirt that made him feel a little possessive. Some may call it a caveman thing to do but so be it.

"It's almost more like a dress on me." she said before going up on her tiptoes to give him a quick kiss.

"It looks sexy as hell on you is what it looks." Riley said. "Feel free to borrow my shirts anytime."

"Is there anything you need me to do. I'm sorry I fell asleep, and you had to do all the work." she apologized.

"It's fine, I promised you I would make dinner, you don't have to do anything. Although if you want to come and sit out here while I cook you can keep me company. It's almost done. The sauce just needs to simmer a little while longer." She followed him into the kitchen, and he pulled out a stool for her to sit on.

"You made the sauce from scratch?" she asked when she saw the remains of some chopped vegetables on his cutting board.

"Yeah, we all had to learn to cook when we were growing up. Pops helped us but he made it clear that we needed to learn to carry our own weight around the house." Riley said. "I actually enjoy cooking for the most part. Granted I wouldn't want to make sauce from scratch every night of the week but it's nice to do it for a special dinner." He smiled at her and she smiled back.

About five minutes later, Riley announced the sauce was ready and told Hannah if she wanted to go sit at the table, he would serve the food. She hadn't noticed the table when she had walked into the kitchen because she had turned toward Riley immediately but when she saw it, she was amazed. It wasn't just set with plates and silverware. There were crystal wine glasses and water glasses. The plates were China and not some plasticware like she used at her house. There was a tablecloth and placemats. It was beautiful. She sat down and when Riley came with the first dish, she told him "This table is beautiful, but you didn't have to do all of this for me, Riley."

"I wanted to. I don't get a lot of company really. When we have family get together, they are usually at Bryan's he has the biggest house and he's sort of been the patriarch of the family for a long time." Riley said. "Besides I needed to impress you so I can convince you to stay and let me make breakfast for you in the morning." He leaned down and gave her a kiss on the cheek before going back to get another dish to bring to the table.

"Well, I will stay on one condition" she teased when he came back. "I get to help with breakfast you don't need to do all of it by yourself."

"But I like spoiling you, Hannah. You always have to take care of Maddie, and lately you've been cooking for me and sometimes for Deke too." Riley said. "Just let me spoil you this weekend. Next time we do this you can totally help."

Hannah just shook her head. She wasn't going to fight with this man, and it was nice that he wanted to spoil her this first time together, but it would have to become more equal at some point or it wasn't going to work.

The dinner was delicious, she couldn't believe he could cook like this and even made the marinara sauce from scratch. When they were done, she did help Riley clear the table and put the dishes in the dishwasher, she wouldn't hear of him having to do all of the work.

"What would you like to do for the rest of our evening, Hannah?" Riley asked. "We can go out on the deck and enjoy the evening, or we can watch a movie or whatever you want. We can go into town too if there's some place you'd like to go."

"I don't want to go anywhere, in fact, I need to run upstairs and wash my under clothes in the sink and hang them to dry, um they got kind of wet." she said with a chuckle.

"That's not a problem, I have a washer and dryer, we can throw anything you want in there. Summer does her laundry here so there's probably some pretty decent smelling soap. I just use the boring stuff."

"If you're sure that's not a problem" she stated.

"No problem at all, it's my insurance policy that you aren't going anywhere for a few hours at least." he said with a smile.

She slapped his chest playfully. "I wasn't going anywhere anyways."

"Why don't we go sit outside for a bit before it gets too dark to see anything and then you can start your laundry after we come back in." Riley sat on the long bench and asked Hannah to come sit on his lap. He made sure she stayed covered, but he put his hand on the soft skin of her hip. "You have the softest skin, Hannah. I've never felt anything so soft." He kissed her deeply. They sat kissing for a long while, but Riley heard a low sound, so he pulled away. He scanned his yard to find the source of the noise.

"What?" Hannah asked. She didn't know why he pulled away.

"There" he whispered softly while pointing toward the tree line.

Hannah looked and saw a fox. She sat mesmerized; she had never seen a fox before except at the local zoo. Oh, this would be such a fun place for Maddie. She could see wildlife like they never had in the city. She needed to slow those thoughts down though. This was her first actual date with Riley, and he may not even be thinking long term at this point. Yes, they had spent hours and hours together in the last several weeks, and he seemed to like kissing her and the sex was definitely great, but he may not be at the point of wanting to take on a wife and a child. "It's so beautiful" she whispered softly so as not to scare it away.

"Not as beautiful as you, Hannah" he whispered in her ear before kissing her on the cheek.

She turned away from the fox to look him in the eye. "You make me feel so special Riley." She leaned in to kiss him on the lips and before long their kisses had turned more heated. She pivoted her body so that she was straddling him on the bench. The t-shirt rode up and her bare flesh was pressed against him. He only had thin shorts on, so it wasn't much of a barrier between them. She could feel him hardening below her and her body wanted that barrier gone. She started to rotate her hips a little and press against him harder.

Finally, Riley couldn't take anymore. He needed to be inside her, but he didn't have condoms down here. He pulled her face away and said, "Slow down sweetheart, I don't have any condoms down here and if you keep up what you are doing, I'm going to lose all control."

"We don't need condoms, I'm on birth control and I trust you. But if you don't think it's private out here, we can definitely go inside." Hannah said.

Hell no, Riley didn't want to go inside. His yard was about as private as it got other than wildlife. Yes, it was possible that someone could go for a walk in the woods, but it was starting to get dark out anyway. "It's private, or as private as any place can be. It's starting to get dark too so that will definitely make it even less likely anyone will see us. But we'll leave your shirt on just in case, so you don't have to worry. It will cover the important parts." Riley shifted so that he could reach his hand under her and pull his shorts down enough to free his cock and pulled her back onto him.

"Besides you have super hearing anyway if you heard that fox." Hannah giggled. "If anyone was out there, I'm pretty sure you would know it." By that time, she had been lowered onto Riley's cock and there weren't any words in her head anymore. As soon as she was fully on his cock, she couldn't help but begin to rotate her hips and move up and down slowly to begin with. She had the shirt on but hadn't bothered with a bra. That gave Riley easy access to her hard beaded nipples through the thin fabric. He rolled them and pinched them. He thought about lifting her shirt so that he could take them in his mouth, but that would pull up the shirt and may not give her the protection he promised she would have. He did have extremely good hearing when he wasn't focused on something else. Rather than take a chance on missing a twig snap or footsteps approaching he used one hand to tease her nipples and squeeze her breasts and the other to hold the back of her shirt down, so they were basically covered. With the motions she was doing, there probably wouldn't be any doubt someone would know what they were doing, but they wouldn't see it. The more Riley played with her nipples, the faster her movements became. She was bouncing up and down much more rapidly now and rotating and rocking on him in almost a dance like fashion. He wasn't sure what her reaction was going to be, but there was something he wanted to try, if she protested at all or acted like she didn't like it, he would stop. He put one finger of the hand holding the shirt down against the tight rosebud of her ass. He didn't insert it, just massaged it around the outer skin. Almost immediately, her orgasm hit her like a tidal wave. Her pussy began milking his cock and he couldn't hold out any longer, he followed her over that wave.

 Hannah collapsed into Riley's chest and just listened to his heart beating. It was fairly rapid, just like hers was. The rhythm began to slow gradually, and it was almost lulling her to sleep within a few short moments. Despite having taken a nap, having a hard orgasm apparently wore her out. She kind of wanted to say something to Riley about what he had done with his finger but wasn't sure how. It had felt amazing and had definitely been the thing that pushed her over that edge. She had never actually had anal sex with anyone, but her husband had done some anal play with her before he had died. She felt herself getting closer and closer to dozing off, so she forced herself to raise up off of Riley's chest. "I should probably get my laundry going soon if it's going to be done before we have to get Maddie in the morning."

 "Okay sweetheart." Riley said. He helped her get to her feet and held her hand until she seemed steady then he got out of the chair and walked into the house.

Hannah headed upstairs to grab her laundry, she asked Riley if he had anything that needed to be washed because her one outfit wouldn't make much of a load and would be a waste of soap and of water.

"Hannah, I don't mind the water usage and I want you to use Summer's soap if you want to, but I don't really want my clothes smelling like lavender or lilies or whatever."

"I don't mind using the regular soap." Hannah said. "I don't use anything really feminine at home either."

"I have a few things in the basket in the closet if you want to do them all." Riley agreed.

Hannah walked down the stairs to the main floor with the basket in hand. "Where's the washing machine?"

"It's in the basement, I can take it down there and get it started." Riley offered.

"Absolutely not" Hannah argued. "You cooked a fabulous meal and have shown me an amazing time. I can handle a load of laundry."

Riley just pointed to the door that led to the basement. He wasn't going to argue with Hannah if she wanted to do the laundry by herself. He poured them each another glass of wine. He wasn't sure if Hannah wanted to stay up long enough to put the clothes in the dryer or if she planned to do that in the morning. They didn't really have a set time to have to go pick up Maddie, so they weren't in any rush. He sat in his living room with the two glasses on the coffee table in front of him.

Chapter Thirteen

It seemed like Hannah had been gone for a long time, so Riley went to make sure she wasn't having a hard time figuring out how to use his washing machine. As he neared the bottom of the stairs, he had a feeling that he knew what was holding her up. He wasn't sure if that was going to be a good thing or a bad thing though. The door to the laundry room was open and so was the door across the hall. The laundry basket sat on the floor in the hallway, still full of their clothing. The light in the room on the left was on, the one on the right, the laundry room was not. This was either going to go really well or really bad. Riley just wasn't sure which.

He continued down to the open doorway and peeked in. Hannah was walking around the room looking at everything. He didn't think he saw any repulsion or fear on her face, but he really wasn't sure what he was seeing. Softly so as to not startle her, he said "Hannah."

Hannah immediately turned at the sound of Riley's voice. She felt like a kid getting caught with her hand in the cookie jar. Riley hadn't given her permission to explore this room. She had seen that the door was slightly ajar, and she just wondered what was in here. What she had found kind of surprised her, but Riley was standing in the doorway with a questioning look on his face, so she owed him an explanation as to what she was doing in here. "Oh, sorry, the door was slightly ajar, and I peeked in here first. The light wasn't on in either room and you hadn't told me which side of the hallway the laundry room was on." She was speaking rapidly, but she was worried he would be upset with her for finding his private things.

"Hannah, it's okay. I don't have anything to hide from you. I haven't told you about this room because honestly, I wasn't sure we were at a place in our relationship to discuss whether or not you knew about or enjoyed BDSM. It's something I enjoy, but not something I have to have if you aren't into it. This door has a lock on it and if it makes you uncomfortable, I'll keep the door locked from now on." he assured.

"It's not a problem for me, but if Maddie ever comes here, this will need to be locked and off limits." Hannah said quietly.

"Of course, Hannah, that's a given." Riley stated. "Right now, though I'm trying to figure out if this repulses you or scares you or intrigues you."

"Um, the last two mostly." Hannah said softly.

"So, you're curious but aren't sure if you would like it." Riley said.

"Right." Hanna agreed.

"Well, like I said, it's something I enjoy but definitely not a deal breaker in a relationship for me. If you ever think you want to explore it, all you have to do is say so. If you never want to do that, that's okay too." Riley said. He hadn't entered the room, he wanted to give Hannah the space to feel comfortable with staying in the room or leaving it.

"I think there are some things I might like to try, but other things I definitely don't want to do." Hannah explained.

"That's a pretty typical response." Riley assured her. "Especially if you've never tried any of it before. Even someone who does have some experience will have things that they don't do. Everyone has their preferences. If there are things you want to try, I'd be happy to introduce you, but that's completely up to when and if you feel ready. I'm curious though, the things you think you might want to try, why do you think that, or how do you know about them?"

"I read romance novels and some of them have BDSM in them." she said.

"Well, honestly I would assume that's a sort of varied way of learning. If they live it or have done their research, it's probably accurate, however I am sure there are some that think they know about it but may not." Riley stated. "So, I would suggest you do your own research, and I don't mean that it has to be done by playing with me. There are lots of ways to learn about it. If you want, I'm sure Sophie would be glad to talk to you about it too."

Hannah looked a little odd at that statement. "You mean they..." she wasn't quite sure how to finish that statement.

"They do or they are, depending on how you were going to finish that statement." Riley went on to assure her "I promise you though that Maddie will never have a clue or see any of their things. Well, except for Bryan's Harley. I've heard they've done some pretty creative things on it, but she won't see anything that would give anything away."

"I'm sure, I trust them to keep Maddie safe, I guess I'm just surprised that I actually know someone who does this." Hannah explained.

"Actually, you probably know a lot more people that do this than you think you do. It's not something people just bring up in normal conversation." Riley said. "Hannah, I'm not going to enter the room unless you want me to, but if there's anything that you want to know what it is or what it does, feel free to ask."

"I'm totally fine with you coming in here Riley, it's your room, and I trust you not to grab me and tie me up and start flogging me." she said rather jokingly but her face got more serious, and she added "although that might be really fun actually." She didn't miss the change in Riley's expression, it was brief before he schooled himself to not react, but it had been there. His nostrils had flared a little bit and there was a definite change in his eyes before he went back to a normal expression. He had stepped into the room though and now his presence seemed to fill the space. Riley wasn't an overly large man, he was muscular but not really bulky, but all of a sudden, the space of the room seemed much smaller to Hannah. Her breathing got heavier, and it almost seemed like some of the oxygen had left the room.

Riley walked slowly toward Hannah, he was going to give her every choice in this process, but he would definitely enjoy tying her up and flogging her. He didn't miss the change in her breathing. The closer he got to her the more it changed, but it wasn't like panic, it was definitely arousal. He stayed far enough away that she wouldn't feel confined, but he reached out a hand and brushed his thumb softly on her cheek. "There is nothing that I would love more than to show you all the amazing things that can be experienced in this room, but until you are sure you're ready I'm not going to push anything, sweetheart."

"I know you won't push me to be ready, Riley and that's a big part of why I think I would want to experience this with you and not someone who was trying really hard to talk me into it." Hannah admitted.

Riley just stood there looking into her eyes trying to read her thoughts. Finally, he realized there was only one way to put this decision fully in her hands and that was to walk away temporarily so that she could think without feeling pressured into doing something that she wasn't ready for. "I'll tell you what, sweetheart. I'm going to go start the load of laundry. While I'm gone, you think about what you want your decision to be. If you want to proceed, by all means I would enjoy that. If you decide you aren't ready, we'll go upstairs and watch a movie or talk or whatever and I will enjoy that time with you too." He looked into her eyes a moment longer hoping that she could see that he was being honest with her. Either activity would be enjoyable because it was time he got to spend with Hannah. He stepped back away from her and left the room to start the laundry. He took his time with the task, he wanted to give Hannah as much time as he possibly could without it seeming like he had disappeared completely.

As soon as Riley had turned to leave the room, Hannah's mind started to race. Did she want to try this? It had been something she had been curious about for years. It wasn't something her husband had any interest in and that had been completely fine. She loved him and what they had done together had always been amazing. But, since his death, she had gotten more and more curious about the things she read in her books. There was no question in her mind that she trusted Riley to not do anything she wasn't comfortable with, and she knew he would stop if she needed him to. Honestly, this was the best time for her to explore her curiosities. Maddie was safely far away; Riley was trustworthy, and he apparently had all of the toys and equipment she had always wondered about. He had what she knew to be a spanking bench because it looked like how they had been described in books. It was sort of like a sawhorse, but not fully. It had a padded shelf for her knees and a shelf that he arms could rest on. It also had places that a chain or hook could be attached to keep the person in position. He had a table that seemed to have similar hooks to bind someone to and there were floggers, canes, crops, and paddles hanging from hooks on the wall. There were some things that she didn't know the name of but that was okay. Riley had seemed willing to teach her and show her what she didn't know. She had a decision to make but really it wasn't a hard one. She had wanted this for years; it was time to go for it. She took off her clothing which really only consisted of Riley's t-shirt, and she folded it and placed it on the shelf that sat along the wall. Riley hadn't given her any specific instructions on that, but it was what she had read many dominants wanted. She didn't know if Riley considered himself a dominant or if he just liked the play aspects of the lifestyle, but she was going to do her best to be submissive to him when they were in this room. She had read about positions, but she had never been in any of them. The one thing that she did remember was that most of them consisted of kneeling in some form, so she got down to her knees and waited for Riley to return.

    When Riley walked back across the hall, at first, he thought Hannah had left the room and gone upstairs. He was surprised that he hadn't heard her footsteps. The stairs were carpeted, but normally he could still hear someone go up or down them. He almost turned to head upstairs to find her when he realized that he was looking too high to see her. She was kneeling beautifully on the floor beside his spanking bench. Oh, some tight ass would complain that she didn't have her form right and she definitely didn't, but for a person who had only ever read about this, she was as perfect as he could ever hope for her to be. It almost took his breath away to see her there. "Hannah, that's the most beautiful thing I have ever seen. I didn't give you any direction when I left, but you took what you know from reading and tried to be pleasing to me and my sweet girl, you definitely have done that." He stepped closer to her and leaned down so he could place a finger under her chin. He lifted her face to his and pierced into her eyes. If he saw anything there that told him she wasn't sure about this, he was going to take a step back. Instead, she looked up at him with the most beautiful soft smile he had ever seen.

"Thank you, Sir." she said softly. "I hoped you would be pleased."

"I am beyond pleased, Hannah. I feel like the luckiest man in the world to be able to introduce you to this."

Hannah had one brief thought and had to know "How many women have you had down here?"

Riley wasn't sure if it was jealousy asking or if she was just curious if he knew what he was doing. "I have had one woman down here a few times, but it's been a couple of years ago. Right after I got home, I started going to some of the local BDSM clubs. I had found some when I was in the military and enjoyed them, so I explored here. At one of the clubs, I met a woman who was a pretty good fit for me as far as BDSM goes. We enjoyed the same things, so we became play partners. However, as much as we enjoyed similar aspects of the lifestyle, we had absolutely nothing in common in what is generally referred to as the vanilla world. So, we played, and yes, we had sex a couple of times, because this stuff can be very arousing, but once our play times were over, she left and went home. We both got to a point that we realized there would never be anything more between us and we both wanted to find someone that we could have the whole package with, so we amicably parted ways."

"Yes, Sir, thank you for answering my question." she said softly.

Riley had to admit he had never heard a sweeter sound in all his life than the sound of his sweet Hannah calling him Sir. He had never really been all that worried about the titles and all of that when he was playing randomly, but to hear the woman that he loved say it made it a very different thing. "God you are so beautiful Hannah, and so perfectly sweet and submissive. With this being your first time, I'm going to go slow and try to explain a little bit, but if you ever have any questions, don't hesitate to ask, or state concerns either. Whatever you need to say is fine. You don't have to try to be quiet. If we continue to pursue this, after you know more about things, I may tell you not to speak at times, but not tonight, Hannah. Tonight, is a learning process for both of us. You are learning about the lifestyle, but I am learning you."

When he put it that way, Hannah knew she had made the right decision, Riley would take the time to teach her. He would listen to every word, every sound, and every breath. He would observe every movement or reaction and he would act accordingly to give her pleasure and never hurt her in a bad way. She was definitely falling in love with this man.

"For starters, do you have any triggers that you know of? For example, does a blindfold scare you? Does being bound by your wrists bring back any bad memories or would wrist be okay but full body not okay because of a past experience? Anything like that that you can think of?"

"No, Riley. I don't have any triggers that I know of and although I have never done it, I have always thought that being tied and at the mercy of someone I trust sounds really hot." Hannah admitted.

"Great, and if you've read those kinds of books, I'm sure you know about a safe word. But tonight, I just want you to be open and talk to me, say 'stop' say 'no' whatever you need to say. If we find that you enjoy this and want to do it again, we'll worry about a safe word and more actual protocol type things. Agreed?" Riley asked.

"Yes, Sir" she said confidently. She hadn't missed the flash that went across Riley's face every time she used the word Sir to him. He hadn't told her she had to use it, but he obviously liked it when she did.

He held his hand out and said, "Let me help you up Hannah." When she was standing, he led her over to the table.

When he had her lay on the table, she realized that it was padded just enough that it wasn't uncomfortable, but it wasn't soft enough anyone would want to sleep on it for long. He had her lay on her stomach and soon she felt a softly lined blindfold being placed over her eyes. She closed her eyes behind the blindfold and tried to clear her mind of anything that would distract her from just feeling the sensations of everything that Riley had in store for her. Next, she felt a soft cuff wrapping around one wrist, it was then fastened to one of the rings on the table. The other wrist was next. When they were both fastened down, Riley said "Hannah, I want you to try to move your arms and try to pull out of the cuffs. I need to know that they aren't too tight, but I also don't want you to slip out of them. Remember if you need them removed at any time just say so."

Hannah did as he had instructed. She could move her arms only slightly and her wrists were definitely not going to come out of the cuffs although they weren't to tight, that they would hinder her circulation.

"All good?" Riley asked.

"Yes, Sir." Hannah replied.

Riley moved down and did the same thing to her ankles, again he had her test them and again he asked if everything was good.

"By the way, I want you to know before we get started, that anything I will use in you or in a sexual way, is brand new. I don't reuse toys from one person to the next." Riley said. With any luck, he would never have to replace the ones he had now because he would be using them on her for the rest of their lives. He had no problem with adding new things if they wanted to try something, but he hoped the things he had were there to stay.

Hannah heard Riley walk across the room to where she knew the floggers and things were hanging. It seemed like an eternity before he came back to the table. Soon though he was softly hitting her back with what had to be a flogger because of the way it hit, but it was so relaxing that it felt like more of a massage than anything else. He moved to her legs and then her ass cheeks, never hitting the same place twice in a row but eventually covering most of her body with the soft thuds. He stepped away again much more briefly this time and came back with something that felt good, but it did leave a small sting behind. At first, Hanna flinched when it hit and every time she did, she felt Riley pause as if he were waiting for her to ask him to stop. She didn't want him to stop though, she just needed to take some time to process it all. After the first several hits, she realized that if she took a deep breath right after she felt the sting and let it out slowly, the small bite of pain turned into something completely different. It turned into pleasure. She knew from her reading that it was most likely endorphins being released but whatever it was it felt amazing if she would just let it.

Riley saw the noticeable change when Hannah went to flinching at the sting to realizing the steps to take to process the pain. At first, he spaced the hits of the flogger out so that she had the time to adjust but as she became faster and faster at processing it and relaxing rather than flinching, he started to pick up the pace. Her skin was turning a beautiful shade of pink. He had no doubt that she would look even more gorgeous as the pink deepened into a light red. But if she couldn't handle that much that was okay too. He was just enjoying giving Hannah her first experience with BDSM. When he was done covering her entire back side with the hits from the second flogger, he sat it down and walked closer to her face. "Hannah, sweetheart, are you still with me?"

"Yes Sir." she said softly.

Riley could tell that she was definitely really getting into all of this, apparently, she did enjoy at least a mild level of pain. "Do you want me to get more intense, or would you rather not?"

"More, please, Sir." Hannah said.

She may claim to have never done anything within the lifestyle before and Riley did believe that she hadn't, but she had definitely taken the stories in those books and learned something. Every time she called him Sir; he fell for her a little more. She was exactly what he had hoped to find in a woman someday. He decided to change things up and try a crop on her to see if she liked the quick slaps it gave. This time, he started on her ass. The fleshiest part of her body. The first slap wasn't really hard, just enough for her to feel it and definitely register that they had moved on to a different type of implement. Her sharp intake of breath made him pause to see how she reacted after. If she recovered quickly, it was most likely just a surprise at the different sensation. If it took longer, she probably wasn't ready for the harder slaps that a crop could give. It took her only seconds to relax fully though so he was pretty sure it had just been the surprise. He used the crop to give three quick slaps on the opposite cheek. She did what she had been doing with the heavier flogger; taking a deep inhale and letting out slowly to let the pain process through her and turn it into a release of endorphins. She obviously was going to be someone that enjoyed at least a moderate amount of pain if she had already figured that out. Endorphins could easily give a submissive a sort of high if they processed them properly if they didn't, it just felt like pain and that wasn't a good thing for most. After a few more swats, Riley decided to turn up the heat in a different way. He walked to the table and opened a small vibrator. He placed it against her clit and turned it to a low speed he laid the remote on the corner near the head so he would be able to reach it easily later. It wouldn't be enough to bring her to orgasm, but it would help push her towards it while he continued to use the crop on her.

Hannah had never felt anything like this in her life. The pain wasn't pain at all anymore, it had morphed into pure pleasure and when Riley had placed the vibrator against her she was definitely getting more and more aroused. Riley continued to use the crop on her buttocks and upper legs for several more hits before she sensed him moving around the table. She could hear his voice from just above her head.

"I want you to take my cock in your mouth Hannah." She opened her mouth and although she couldn't see him, she felt him guide her to his steel hard cock. She willingly allowed him to fuck her mouth while she still felt the crop slapping the flesh of her ass. The speed of the vibrator went up a few notches, Riley must have a remote because he hadn't had to touch it. Her body felt like it was pure sensation, her brain couldn't focus on any one thing. Every time she tried to focus on Riley's cock going in and out of her mouth, he would give her another swat with the crop. Giving oral to a guy had always been a huge turn on to her too, especially if he was the one in control of the depth and speed. But with the added slaps of pain and a vibrator buzzing rapidly on her clit she wasn't going to last much longer.

Riley could tell by Hannah's body movements, as restricted as they were with the cuffs, that she was getting close to orgasm and so was he. He guided the crop right for the slit between her ass cheeks and slapped it against her. She tried to yell out, but his cock was deep in her throat pulsing with his release, apparently that combination put her over the edge too and she was orgasming. Riley had come so hard that he had to brace himself with his hands on the corner of the table for a minute to get his breathing back to normal and his head back on straight. He clicked off the remote to the vibrator so that it wouldn't continue to push her to another possible orgasm. He didn't remember ever coming so hard from oral, but he wanted both of their next orgasms to come while he was deep inside her. He unfastened her wrist and then her ankles. He took the blindfold off and then scooped her up from the table. He carried her up the two flights of stairs to his bedroom and laid her on his bed. "If you are to sore or whatever, I totally understand, but I would really like to make love to you right now, Hannah." Riley said.

Hannah didn't think she would ever be too sore to want to have Riley inside her. She was amazed at his strength and his stamina. He had just had a huge orgasm in his playroom and then he carried her up two flights of stairs and he was ready to go again apparently. "Yes Riley, I want that too, I'm not sore."

No sweeter words had ever been spoken in Riley's opinion. He laid next to her on the bed and began kissing her. He was hard and ready to go in no time at all, but he wanted to be sure that she was too. He kissed her deeply, their tongues dancing in an erotic tango and he began stroking her clit. She was still wet from the orgasm she had downstairs, but Riley still wanted to make her feel amazing. She was soon squirming and trying to pull him on top of her. He took her hint and moved over her, slowly letting his cock sink into her warmth. He wanted to take this one slow and easy because despite the fact that she said she wasn't sore, Riley was pretty sure she would be feeling the effects of all of their lovemaking and time in his playroom in the morning. He stroked in and out slowly softly telling her all the things he wanted her to know. "You amaze me, Hannah. You're so beautiful. I admire your strength." Lots of little sentences and praises, but just before his orgasm hit him, his last words to her were "I think I'm falling in love with you, Hannah."

Hannah had heard Riley's words, every single one of them. When he said he thought he was falling in love, she realized that she was too. She just didn't know if she could say it yet. For her it wasn't just a matter of whether or not she loved Riley, she had a daughter to consider. She knew that Maddie loved Riley, but she didn't know if her daughter was ready for a new father figure in her life. A long term relationship wasn't something she could just decide to do. Maddie would have at least a small say in anything Hannah did for close to another decade. She didn't want to say that she loved him, although she knew in her heart that she did. But she didn't want him to think that she hadn't heard him or was ignoring the comment, so she did the only thing she could think to do and that was to shut him up with a deep hard kiss as they both reached the amazing bliss of an orgasm.

Riley didn't mind that Hannah hadn't immediately returned the sentiment he had expressed. He understood that it was way more complicated for her. She had been married before, so she might still feel that it was too soon after his death. She had a child to take into consideration. He wasn't going anywhere any time soon, she had time to sort out what her feelings were and how Maddie would feel about a possible relationship between them. He rolled off of her and looked back at the bed and said "I'm going to start a hot bath for you because despite the fact that you say you don't hurt anywhere, you have had more sex in a matter of hours than you've had in a long time, plus you've had your first experience with floggers and crops. Not to mention the fact that you were bound in one position for quite a while. I'll get it going and then go downstairs and swap the laundry over and make sure everything is locked up and shut down."

"Thank you, Riley." Hannah said.

"Nothing to thank me for Hannah, I'm sure I enjoyed it just as much if not more than you did." He walked into his large bathroom and began running hot water into the massive tub. He tested it to make sure it wasn't too hot and then he looked in the cupboard where Summer kept some of her things and found some bath beads. He smelled them and they smelled like peppermint or something, not too girly so he poured some in. He had no idea how many you were supposed to put in there, but he put in a good sprinkle. He then headed downstairs to make sure the doors were locked, and the alarm system was turned on. He didn't really feel the need for the alarm system, his house didn't really look like the type most people would try to rob, but he had a brother that was a tech genius and a little paranoid, so they all had alarm systems and he would bitch if they didn't get set. Of course, now, Trevor would know that Riley was at his own house and not at Hannah's which would also mean he would know that Hannah was spending the night with Riley because he wouldn't have left her home alone while guarding her. That didn't bother him, Trevor might give him shit about it, but it would all be in fun. His brother already knew they were at least dating since they had seen him earlier.

Hannah made her way into Riley's bathroom, and this was the first time she had noticed the massive bathtub. When she had come in here earlier, she had used the sink and the toilet. The tub was in an alcove of sorts and unless you walked around the partial wall you didn't really see it. The thing looked about as big as her whole bathroom at home. There was an amazing smell coming from it too. Riley must have put some oil or bath salts into the water. She leaned down to check the water temperature before stepping in and she found that just like everything else Riley did, it was the perfect temperature. She sank down into the tub and she had to admit that Riley had been right, she wasn't really sore per se, but she could tell she would end up achy if she didn't soak in this tub for a while. When Riley walked back into the room, she only then realized that he had put his shorts back on. "You got dressed? I thought maybe you would join me since I'm pretty sure it could hold half a dozen people." she teased.

"Not half a dozen, I've never tried it but I'm pretty sure it can fit two though." He dropped his shorts to the floor and got in the tub. He worked his way around, so he was sitting behind Hannah. When he was seated, he pulled her back towards him so her back was laying against his chest.

"It smells wonderful and it's a very relaxing scent, but I'm surprised you have peppermint bath salts." Hannah said.

"Oh, I don't, Summer does though." Riley said

"She has lots of things here, does she come over often?" she asked.

"Well, she has a tiny one bedroom house and therefore a tiny bathroom and no laundry facilities. Most of the time I'm either not here because I'm working or even if I am here, I don't mind her using them. It's not like it's an inconvenience. She's my big sister and I like that I can give her things she needs. She took care of me for years, it's my way of starting to pay her back I guess."

Hannah knew for sure she was falling in love with Riley, actually she was pretty sure she was past the point of falling and was at the fallen stage. She lay back against him and just relaxed.

Riley took the washcloth he had set out for her and slowly began washing her arms and her stomach and chest. He nudged her to lean forward so that he could wash her back. He gave her the washcloth to finish washing whatever she needed to wash. He wasn't going to attempt to wash her pussy because he wasn't sure how tender it might be, and he definitely wasn't going to risk starting something with her again. He would be perfectly content to sit here and hold her until she was ready to get out.

Hannah finished washing herself and then lay back against Riley's chest. She was starting to doze off, so she told him she was going to get out. Riley stood up and helped her out of the tub. He wrapped a big soft towel around her and helped her dry off.

Riley could tell that Hannah was about half asleep so as soon as he got her dry, he scooped her up and carried her to bed. He laid her on the side closest to the bathroom and went around and crawled in beside her. She immediately rolled into him and put her head on his chest and was asleep in seconds. Sleep didn't come as fast for Riley, but when he did fall asleep it was a deep sleep. He hadn't slept in his big comfortable bed in weeks because he had been staying with Hannah.

Chapter Fourteen

In the morning, Riley woke before Hannah did but he had to admit having her next to him had given him the best nights sleep he had in as long as he could remember. He tried to gently move from under her since she was still laying half on him, but she started to stir.

"What time is it?" she asked groggily.

"It' just after nine. You have plenty of time to rest." Riley assured her. "I'm going down to start a pot of coffee. But I won't start breakfast until you're ready."

"Okay, sounds good." Hannah said rolling back over to the warm side of the bed Riley had just vacated. When she did, the sheet had fallen a little and Riley noticed a few small bruises on her ass cheeks. They didn't look like they would be a problem, but if they were, he would keep it milder when they played again. And he was sure they would be in his room again, at some point. It may not be right away because of the logistics of having Maddie around, but it would happen again, at least if he had anything to say about it.

He threw on a clean pair of shorts and made his way down to the kitchen to start a pot of coffee. When it was done, he took a cup and went to sit on the back deck. He spent a lot of time out here when the weather would allow it. He liked the feeling of wide open spaces. Ever since the incident in Iraq, small spaces seemed to bother him. He thought it might be because he knew that most of his teammates had most likely been crushed to death, but any who hadn't probably died of injuries sustained when they got trapped in small pockets left by the falling debris. After all, they hadn't found Nate because there was so much debris and it was unsafe to try to move some of it. About a half hour later, Hannah came padding out with bare feet and another of his t-shirts on. She had a cup of coffee in her hand. She sat on the chair next to his.

"This coffee is amazing." Hannah said taking a small sip. She looked around at the yard and it hadn't gotten any less amazing than it was the night before. She would love to have a yard like this.

Riley looked at her and a little hesitantly asked "How are you this morning Hannah?"

"I'm fine, why?" she was puzzled by his question.

"Well, when you rolled over in the bed, I noticed you have some bruises on you and I wanted to make sure you were okay."

"Oh, yeah, I'm fine Riley. I felt a little twinge, so I looked in the full-length mirror. I think I would have been more surprised if I didn't have them than I would have been that I did." Hannah said.

"But you're, okay?" he asked.

"I'm fine, Riley." She stood up and sat her coffee down on the table. She walked over to him and sat on his lap. He gladly shifted to give her room to sit. "What we did last night was amazing. I've always wondered and now I know. Thank you for showing me and I hope we get the chance to explore more in the future." She leaned in and kissed him.

"As long as you're sure you're okay." Riley said.

"I'm fine, although I have to admit it's been hours since we ate and all the physical activity since then has me starving." she said with a smile.

Riley leaned in and kissed her again and then said, "I'll go get breakfast started."

Hannah stood up and said "Nonsense, I'm helping you don't need to wait on me Riley. We can do it together.

Riley made a ham, cheese, and onion omelet while Hannah made toast and cut up some fruit. Riley thought they made a pretty good team in the kitchen. He was pretty sure he was going to ask Hannah to marry him someday when he thought all three of them were ready.

After breakfast they cleared the dishes and Hannah went downstairs to get the laundry. When she came back upstairs, she said. "I should probably go home and change before we pick up Maddie. I don't know if it will confuse her or not if I'm wearing the same clothes, but I don't want to take a chance on her bringing up questions I'm not able to answer right now."

"Sure, we'll head for your place anytime you want to." Riley said. "I'll go change and be ready whenever you are."

When Riley left, Hannah picked up her phone to check for messages. There was a text from Maddie.

Mom, I'm having so much fun! Can I spend the night here again sometime?

Sure, Maddie, I'll see what Sophie and Bryan say.

Moments later, came another text.

They say yes, Mommy!

Well, I'll talk to them when I get there.

Hannah had to smile at her daughter's motivation, if she wanted something there was little chance of stopping her unless it was something bad for her. Apparently, they didn't have to be in any rush to pick her up, she was having a great time. Hannah had worried that she might get a call in the middle of the night that Maddie had woken up in a strange place and wanted to go home.

When Riley came back downstairs, he saw Hannah looking at her phone with a smile. "Everything okay?"

"Yeah, that was Maddie. She had a great time and already wants to do it again." Hannah stated.

"Great, I'm sure Sophie and Bryan will be glad to have her. Is there anything you want to do today before we go pick her up or are you anxious to go get her? Riley asked.

"Well, I was going to say I wanted to pick her up because I'm surprised, she made it through the night on her first sleepover, but since she seems to be having fun, there is one thing I'd like to do." Hannah said.

"What's that, sweetheart?"

"I'd like to go for a motorcycle ride. I've never been on one." Hannah stated.

"By all means. My bike is down at Triskelion, but we'd have to go there anyway to get you a helmet, so that all works out." Riley said. "Are you ready to go?"

"I just have to put on my shoes."

They headed out the door and got in Riley's big truck. When they got to the motorcycle shop, Riley went in and picked out a helmet that would fit Hannah. When they got on his motorcycle, he asked "Is there anywhere special you'd like to go?"

"Not really, just somewhere that you can ride faster than in the city. If I'm going to experience it, I might as well get the full effect." Hannah said.

Riley pulled out of the shop and headed out of town so they could ride the rolling hills of the countryside. He had been right, the only thing that was about as enjoyable as her in front of him on a horse was having her behind him on his Harley. He never went over the speed limit, but he went as fast as was allowed. He liked the feeling of Hannah wrapping her arms tightly around him. He had asked her a few times if she was okay with the speed and she said she was, so he kept riding. When they were about twenty miles outside of town, Riley slowed down so he could ask her a question. "It would take about an hour to get to Pop's Diner. Do you want to head there and grab lunch before we go back to your place for you to change?"

That sounded good to Hannah, so she gave him a smile and a nod. Riley had purposely ridden in a direction that was away from the diner rather than towards it hoping that by the time he took the ride back they could enjoy lunch at the diner. For some reason, it was important to him that Pops knew he had a relationship with Hannah and that the two liked each other. He had taken Maddie and Hannah both there, but by taking Hannah alone it would give her and the older man a chance to get to know each other more. Riley remembered things about his parents, but not a lot, for the most part Pops had been the only parental figure in Riley's life.

They had a good meal and nice conversation with Pops. Just as they were getting ready to leave, Pops looked at Riley and said, "You hang on to this one young man, you don't let a good woman like her go."

Riley blushed at the man's forwardness and so did Hannah, but he didn't let the embarrassment stop him from saying "That's the plan, Pops." That comment made Hannah blush even more. When they got out to the motorcycle, Riley stopped and tilted Hannah's face up to his. "I hope that didn't embarrass you too much, Hannah, but I agree with Pops, I hope to keep you around for a long time if you'll have me." Hannah looked like she didn't know what to say, so Riley clarified, "No, Hannah, that's not a proposal, not yet. We're not ready for that and if we were, that one would have sucked. But I don't plan on going anywhere anytime soon."

Hannah just smiled and nodded. Riley leaned in for a kiss and then they got on the bike to ride to her house to change. They would have to switch vehicles back too so they would have room for Maddie.

When they arrived at Bryan's house, they could hear voices in the back yard, so they just headed around the side of the house instead of knocking on the door. Maddie was racing around the yard with Sempre Fi close behind. Every few minutes, Maddie would slow and let the puppy catch up with her so they could tumble in the grass. When she spotted her mother and Riley, she ran to them, and the puppy followed. "Mommy, Riley!" she exclaimed. "I had so much fun. Please let me come back again."

"We'll see." Hannah said, "Were you a good girl for Sophie and Bryan?"

"I was mommy. I ate all of my regular food before I had a cupcake, and I went to bed when they told me too and guess what?" the little girl was talking a mile a minute.

"Sophie and Fi and me had a sleep over in the living room, we made a tent and everything." Maddie said.

"That sounds like a lot of fun." Riley said.

"It was, it was so much fun. I wish we had a bigger living room so we could make a tent there."

"Well, maybe we can make a tent under the kitchen table." Hannah offered.

"Yes, mommy, please!"

"We will, but not tonight, tonight is a school night. But maybe another weekend." Hannah offered.

"Yay!" Maddie was off running again.

"Sorry, we tried to wear her out for you" Sophie laughed.

"I'm sure by the time she gets home and has dinner and a bath the exhaustion will set in." Hannah said. "I really appreciate you keeping her like this."

"Anytime, we loved having her here." Bryan said putting his arm around his fiancé. "We aren't ready for kids of our own yet, but we love having Maddie here."

They visited with Bryan and Sophie for a little while and then decided to grab a pizza to take home for dinner. By the time they got home Maddie was barely able to eat her pizza before falling asleep. They tucked her into bed and then Riley gave Hannah a quick kiss goodnight before heading to the couch. He wasn't really tired because of the good amount of sleep he had gotten the night before, so he decided to watch a movie on his iPad to wind down.

Hannah was sleeping soundly when she heard a loud gut wrenching scream in the living room. She heard Riley's loud "NNNOOOOOO" and went running out to see what was happening. She could see him thrashing on the couch and mumbling in his sleep. She walked over to him to try to wake him up and comfort him. "Riley, it's okay, you're here in my living room. Wake up Riley."

Riley sat up so quickly that he knocked Hannah back a few steps. He was having a hard time figuring out what was going on until he saw the look of concern on Hannah's face and then saw Maddie standing in the hallway peering out at him. Fuck, he had one of his nightmares and now both of them were terrified of him. He stood up and walked toward the door. Hannah tried to stop him and all he could say was "I just need some air." Then he walked out to his truck and got inside. He picked up his cell phone and called his brother Trevor.

"What's up, Rye?" Trevor said. "It's really late, is something wrong?"

"You could say that." Riley began. "I had one of my nightmares and I scared the shit out of Hannah and Maddie. I need to get out of here, but I can't leave them alone. The guy is in jail awaiting sentencing, but we all know it ain't over till he's locked up for good. Could you come and keep an eye on the house till Deke gets here in a few hours. I just need some space."

"I'll be right there." Trevor said.

Riley was glad that his brother didn't say 'I told you so'. Both of his brothers had been worried that he couldn't take this assignment. Apparently, they were right. He wasn't ready for assignments from BACA, and he definitely wasn't ready to have a relationship with a woman and her young child.

Hannah took Maddie back to her room and tucked her in again. "Is Riley okay, mommy?"

"He will be, he just had a bad dream. You know how those are, sometimes you don't know what's real and what isn't, and it just takes some time to calm down. Riley will be fine. You try to go back to sleep."

"Okay mommy." Maddie rolled over and cuddled back into her bed.

Hannah went to look out the front window to see if she could see where Riley was. She wanted to go out and talk to him to make sure he was okay. Just as she was ready to go out there, she saw another truck pull up in front of the house and Riley's brother Trevor got out of it. At least he had called someone that he could talk to. She went back to bed, she didn't want to interrupt whatever it was that Riley needed from his brother, but she didn't fall asleep for a long while waiting to hear Riley come back in the house.

"Hey, Rye." Trevor said as he walked up. "You, okay?"

"Yeah, you know, just the same ole same ole. I just can't go back in there right now. I saw how badly I scared them. I guess you and Bryan were right, I'm not ready for this. Can you make sure they're taken care of or if you can't do it, maybe they can stay at Bryan's. Maddie really likes it there." Riley said.

"I'll stay, but I really think you need to go back in there and talk to Hannah. I'm pretty sure she has feelings for you. She deserves to hear it from you." Trevor stated.

"I know, I just can't right now." Riley said. He thanked his brother and got in his truck and drove away.

Hannah had finally drifted off to sleep and when her alarm went off, she quickly went to the living room to find Riley, but he wasn't there. She looked out the window and saw Trevor's truck, but not Riley's. She ran back to her room and threw on some clothes. She made her way out to Trevor's truck. He saw her coming and got out to talk to her. "Where's Riley?" she asked.

"He just needed some time to think. He said his bad dream scared you two and he needed some time to process it. I'm not sure what he's told you about his past, but he was in Iraq…" Trevor began.

"Yeah, and he rescued a little girl from a building but then it collapsed and trapped all of his team." Hannah finished for him.

"Wow, that's more than he's ever told any of us. We know it all because Bryan knew some people that were high enough up that they could get the information for him, but Riley has never actually told anyone to my knowledge except maybe the shrink he saw for a long time." Trevor sounded surprised that she knew so much.

"When will he be coming back?" Hannah asked.

"He didn't say, he just asked that I stay here and work with Deke to cover you guys until he gets back." Trevor stated.

Hannah stood there for long minutes sorting things out in her brain. Finally, she said "You and Deke can figure out the best way to get Maddie to school, whatever she is comfortable with is fine with me. I'm not going to work today; I want to be here when Riley gets back." She turned and walked back to the house to get Maddie ready for school. She would explain that Riley had needed to take care of some things, so he had asked his brother to come be with them for a bit. She would let Maddie go to school with whichever one of them she felt more comfortable with.

Trevor watched Hannah walk away. The problem was, he wasn't sure how long Riley would be gone. He was out running from some ghosts that weren't ever going to stop chasing him until he figured out how to get rid of them.

Maddie was fine with riding to school with Deke, she said she understood why Riley had needed to have some time, she had had bad dreams before and sometimes you just needed to go somewhere and think.

Every time Hannah heard a car out on the road, she looked out the window to see if it was Riley and every time, she saw Trevor's truck out front but no other vehicle in her yard.

By Wednesday, Hannah realized that Riley wasn't coming back, at least not any time soon and she couldn't keep missing work hoping for a chance to talk to him. She had called and it always went to voicemail, so he had his phone turned off. She had sent texts hoping that maybe at some point he would at least turn the phone on to check them. She was finding it harder and harder to answer Maddie's questions about when Riley would be back because she honestly didn't know and although she told her daughter that, it wasn't a good enough answer for the little girl, and Hannah didn't blame her for feeling that way, it wasn't a good enough answer for her either. But there wasn't really anything she could do.

When Riley had pulled out of Hannah's driveway, he wasn't really sure where he was heading. He went to Triskelion and got on his bike and just started out of town. He couldn't get the look of terror on Maddie's face out of his head. She had already been through so much; she didn't need a man who was supposed to be her protector scaring her even more. By the time he got out of town he had made a decision on where to go. He headed for the small cabin on a lake about a hundred miles north of Grand Rapids. He had grown up going there with his family and they were all allowed to use it whenever they wanted. Technically their parents had left it to Bryan because he was the oldest, but they had always told them it was for the whole family to use and enjoy. When he got to the small town the cabin was near, he stopped at the grocery store and bought some supplies that would last him several days. He wasn't sure how long it was going to take to be able to face anyone again after the things he had done. He had practically knocked Hannah on the ground, and he had scared Maddie to death. Yeah, that was a really good way to start a relationship.

Chapter Fifteen

By Friday, Hannah had decided it was time to make a bigger effort to work things out with Riley. She called Sophie and asked if she and Bryan could stop by the next morning. They agreed to be there by nine.

When they arrived, Hannah greeted them at the door and asked, "Sophie would you mind taking Maddie out into the backyard to play, I need to talk to Bryan."

"Sure" Sophie said. When they walked in the door, she spotted the little girl sitting on the couch watching cartoons. "Hey Maddie, do you want to go out in the back yard with me?"

"Sure." Maddie said with none of her usual excitement. She got up and followed Sophie out into the yard though.

As soon as Maddie was out of ear shot, Hannah turned to Bryan. "Okay, where is he?"

"I promise you Hannah, I don't know. I haven't heard from him either." Bryan stated.

"You may not know, but you have some ideas, I drove out to his house, his truck isn't there." she said.

"No, it's at Triskelion, he took his bike." Bryan said.

"Where would he go, I need something." Hannah said with tears in her eyes. "He told me he was falling in love with me, and I'm already in love with him. I can't let something as stupid as a nightmare be what ruins that."

Bryan looked at her for a moment and he could see the love in her eyes. "Hang on." He pulled out his cell phone and said "Trevor, get in here."

A minute later, Trevor came in the door. "What's up?"

"We need to help Hannah find our dumb ass brother." Bryan said.

"Well, his cell is off, so there's no signal to trace, I've been checking." Trevor said. "He didn't take the truck, so the GPS system is no help."

Bryan was pretty sure his techie brother knew more than he was saying but didn't want to rat Riley out if he really didn't want to be found. "Look, Riley told Hannah he's in love with her, and she feels the same way about him. We both know this is the PTSD talking and the only thing that's going to help him get past that is love and support. If you know anything, tell Hannah, she deserves to know."

Trevor hesitated for a few more moments looking back and forth between Hannah and his brother. Finally, he could see exactly what Bryan had been talking about, there was so much love and so much hurt in the woman's eyes. He looked at Bryan and said, "The security system alerted me from the cabin the day he left."

"Is he still there?" Bryan asked.

Trevor pulled out his phone and tapped on somethings and then held up his phone to his brother.

Hannah looked at the phone too and saw Riley from the back of his head, it looked like he was sitting on a deck or porch of some kind looking out at a lake or pond. "That's him! You've got to tell me where this is." she exclaimed.

Bryan wrote down the address and told her it was about a hundred miles north. It would take her a couple of hours to get there because it wasn't on a main highway.

"I know it's a lot to ask, but would you and Sophie be willing to take Maddie to your house for however long it takes for me to talk some sense into him?" Hannah begged.

"I'm sure Sophie would love that and if talking doesn't knock any sense into him, let me know and Trevor and I will come up there and knock it into him another way." Bryan smiled.

Hannah made her way out to the backyard to talk to her daughter. "Maddie, I need to go away for a little while, it may just be today, or it may be more days. I'm not sure right now, but Bryan said he and Sophie would like to have you stay at their house until I get back. Is that okay?"

"It's okay Mommy, but where are you going?" Maddie asked.

"I'm going to find Riley and talk to him and see if I can get him to come back." Hannah stated. She didn't miss the fact that Sophie looked at her and gave her a big smile.

"Yay! Mommy. Please find him and tell him that he needs to come home. Anyone can have bad dreams, but the best way to get rid of them is lots of love and lots of hugs and kisses. And if he has any more bad dreams, we will hug him and make them go away." Maddie said with complete sincerity. It was pretty obvious that the little girl was in love with Riley too.

"I'll do that Maddie, let's go pack your suitcase so you can go to Sophie's house." They packed her things and after she left, Hannah threw a bag together for herself. She was going to find him, and she wasn't going to leave until he agreed to come back home with her. No matter how long that took.

Riley heard the car pull up and he had a feeling he knew who it was. It was a car and not a truck, therefore it wasn't one of his brothers. It was possible that it was Summer, but his bet was on it being Hannah. He knew his brother Trevor would know where he was because the security system had alerted him to the fact that someone was at the cabin. The cameras would show him who it was. He heard the footsteps and knew for sure it was Hannah. He knew the sound of her shoes compared to the ones Summer usually wore. He didn't turn to look at her, he wasn't sure he could face her after what he had done to her.

"Hey Riley." Hannah said as she approached him "We've missed you."

"I just think you're better off without me around." Riley said. That was the way to go, make a clean break of it. They both knew that he was messed up, they didn't need to talk about it. They could just go their separate ways and not have to go into just how much of a disaster he was.

"Well, I don't agree and neither does Maddie." Hannah said.

Riley glanced up slightly, he hadn't heard Maddie's footsteps, but if she was here, he was going to do everything in his power for her to not have any reason to fear him any more than she already did. Fortunately, she wasn't there.

"Why did you leave, Riley. You told me last weekend that you were in love with me and then you just take off and disappear." Hannah said.

Riley could hear the tears in her voice, and he was really sorry that he had made her cry, but it was better than hurting her physically or making her live in fear of him. "I can't live with myself for scaring you and Maddie. I just thought it was better if I left."

"You didn't scare Maddie, Riley." Hannah began. "You may have startled her like any loud noise would in the middle of the night. If a tree branch fell, she would have been just as startled. What is scaring her is the fear that you won't come back."

"She's a kid, she doesn't realize that it's better if I don't"

"Well, I'm an adult and I realize that it isn't better if you don't." Hannah began. "See, where I come from, people who are in love and building a relationship talk about stuff and work it out. They don't just walk away and hide."

"But I'm a mess, Hannah." Riley explained. "It's not your job to deal with my mess."

"Why not?" Hannah asked indignantly. "You dealt with my mess."

"That's not the same. You and Maddie needed protecting by no fault of your own." Riley stated.

"And you need help dealing with your nightmares. Those are no fault of your own either Riley. You didn't make that building collapse." Hannah said. "You were there following orders from your superiors. It went bad and lot of people suffered because of it. But that's not on you."

Riley sat silently for a long while just letting Hannah's words flow through his mind. Finally, when he spoke, it was barely above a whisper. "There were times that I wished I had died. There are times that I feel guilty because I survived, and they didn't." He was still staring out over the calm water of the lake.

Hannah walked over to Riley and placed a hand on his shoulder, "Oh, Riley, I am so glad you didn't die over there. I would have never gotten to meet you and fall in love with you."

He finally looked at Hannah "How can you love me, I hurt you."

"The only thing you did that hurt me was not come back and talk to me about what was going on. You said you needed air and walked out. I've been waiting every day for you to get enough air that you could come back." Hannah cried.

"I almost knocked you over." Riley lamented.

"Almost, yes, but that was just as much my fault. I should have known not to get so close to you when you were having a nightmare. I just wanted to wake you up and make it go away." They both sat quietly for long minutes before Hannah added. "You know what Maddie told me when I told her I was going to try to find you? She told me to tell you that it was time for you to come home. She said that anyone can have bad dreams but the only way to make them go away is lots of love and hugs and kisses. And if you ever have a bad dream again, she will be there to hug you and make them go away."

"She's just a kid, she doesn't understand what could happen." Riley explained.

"Well, she may be a kid, but she definitely understands a lot of things. She knows she misses you and that's all that matters to her. She prays for you every night when she says her bedtime prayers. She asks God to keep you safe wherever you are and to help you come back home safely. She cries every night because she misses you." Hannah couldn't keep the tears out of her eyes.

"I just can't come back right now, Hannah. I have to get this fixed." Riley said.

"Okay then." Hannah said sitting in the chair next to him. "I promised my daughter that I would do everything I could to bring you back home with me. I'm not in any hurry. Maddie is safe with Sophie and Bryan for however long this takes. I'll stay here and wait for you to sort it out, or I'll help you sort it out. Either way, I'm not leaving."

Riley sat there in silence for a long time it had probably been at least an hour when he asked "Why?"

"Why what Riley?" Hannah asked softly.

"Why do you want me to come back? Why do you want to be with someone that's going to freak out in the middle of the night in your house?"

"Well, for one, you've been with us for weeks and last night was the first bad dream. I don't know what led to that, but it's also something I'm willing to help you with in any way I can.: Hannah said. She thought she heard Riley mumble something, so she asked, "What did you say?"

"You didn't wish me sweet dreams. I know it sounds stupid or whatever, but this is the first night that I have fallen asleep without you wishing me sweet dreams." Riley said softly.

Hannah stood up and walked over to Riley. She climbed up on his lap, which wasn't easy because he hadn't been sitting in a position that he was prepared for her, but she was pretty certain that he also wouldn't let her fall. She had been right, he shifted and gave her space, he put his hands on her to make sure she didn't fall. "Oh, Riley." She leaned in and kissed him on the cheek. "If that's what you think keeps your bad dreams away, I'll say it every night from now on and if I forget, you remind me. But the biggest reason I want you to come back is that I love you and Maddie does too." She had tears streaming down her face, and Riley had a few of his own. He wrapped her tightly against him and she leaned into him and just let him hold her for however long it took for him to be ready to let go.

Hannah wasn't sure how long she had been in Riley's lap, but she had apparently dozed off because his standing up with her in his arms woke her slightly. "Sorry" she tried to shift but he held her even tighter.

"It's okay, Hannah." Riley said. "I was going to go put you on a bed so you can sleep."

"I haven't slept much this week, but by the looks of your eyes, you haven't either." Hannah said.

"No, but I'm used to that. I stay awake a lot so that I don't have dreams." Riley stated.

"Then I'll lay down, but only if you join me." Hannah protested.

"I'll lay with you for a bit if that will help you be able to fall asleep." Riley promised. He would keep himself awake until she fell asleep and then come back out here and sit. He felt bad that he had been the reason that she hadn't been sleeping.

Riley laid her on the bed and then lay beside her. She rolled into him and stroked his cheek. When he looked her in the eyes, she said softly "Sweet dreams, Riley." She closed her eyes and fell asleep against him.

Riley was afraid to fall asleep, but she had wished him sweet dreams so maybe he could. He also realized that the night they had slept in his bed she hadn't wished him sweet dreams, but she had been there beside him. Maybe her presence would have the same effect. It was worth a try; she had said she wanted him to sleep. He was still worried that he would wake in a nightmare, but this time at least Hannah would know what was going on and hopefully she could move away when he started thrashing before she got hurt. Despite his exhaustion, it still took him a long time to let himself fall asleep, but finally, a deep sleep came.

Hannah woke up because her stomach was growling. It was dark in the cabin, so night must have fallen. She looked over at Riley who was sleeping peacefully next to her. She didn't want to disturb his sleep, so she forced herself to lay still beside him longer. Whatever it took for Riley to be okay was fine with her. She wasn't going anywhere until she convinced him to come back with her. She drifted back to sleep apparently because she woke again when Riley started moving to try to get out of bed without waking her up. "What time is it?"

"It's early morning, the sun is starting to come up." Riley replied. He laid back down and put his arm back around her.

"Wow, we slept a long time." Hannah said. "I guess we were both super tired."

"I realized something just before I fell asleep last night Hannah." Riley said. "I realized that the night you stayed at my house, you didn't tell me sweet dreams, but you were in my arms. So, I think having you next to me makes the dreams stay away too. I slept like a baby last night."

"Well, I'm not going anywhere. With Maddie I'm not sure we can sleep together without her figuring something out, but I will definitely do one of the two." Hannah assured. "And, even if you do have a bad dream, trust us to still love you through it and be there to help you."

Riley still had a lot of thinking to do. He understood that Hannah thought they could help him with his nightmares, but if something happened and he hurt either one of them physically or emotionally, he wouldn't be able to live with himself.

Hannah could still feel some tension in Riley as they prepared coffee and breakfast together, so she decided that she wasn't going to talk about going home until he was ready to talk about it. Between Bryan and Sophie, Trevor, and Deke, she knew her daughter was in good hands, and they would get her to school on Monday if Hannah wasn't back by then. She had texted them when she pulled into the driveway at the cabin and told them she had arrived safely. Sophie had texted back that they were all good on that end and Maddie was welcome to stay as long as she needed to.

The strained silence was too much for Hannah, she realized that Riley was still trying to sort it all out in his head and she wasn't going to pressure him to do that any faster, but she couldn't just sit there and not talk either. So, she asked him about the cabin and asked stories about the times he had come there as a kid. Riley seemed happier than he had been since she got here when he was sharing memories of his childhood, so she kept asking him more and more about those memories. They spent the whole day sharing memories and talking about everything and yet nothing important for anything other than to get to know each other.

It was early evening, and they were again sitting on the porch watching the water. There were ducks and geese that often swam past or landed on the water. Fish jumped and birds swooped down to grab a fish now and then. Hannah had seen a bird she didn't recognize, and Riley told her it was a loon. She had seen an eagle and several hawks too. This would be another place she would love to bring Maddie if Riley ever got his demons banished and decided to come home. She wasn't going to push him though; she was going to let him work it out with her help if he wanted it. She also wasn't going to make love with him again though. She couldn't go there if he wasn't going to be around anymore.

They enjoyed a nice dinner at a small restaurant in the little town and then went back to the cabin. It was fairly remote, they had cell signal but there wasn't any cable or anything for the television, and Hannah was fine with that. If they sat and watched TV, they could both become mindless and never get to the heart of the problems at hand. They did a lot of talking, but they also had long times of silence. But it never seemed awkward to Hannah. When it came time for them to go to bed, Hannah asked, "Is there another bed that I can sleep in?"

Riley could fully understand why she wouldn't want to take the chance of sleeping with him again. The night before they had both been exhausted, but tonight he would be more likely to have a nightmare if he was going to have one. "Yeah, sure, you can take the room we had last night, and I'll sleep down the hall in one of the other rooms."

Before he could walk away, Hannah stopped him for two reasons, she was pretty sure that he was thinking that her reasoning was because she was afraid, he would have a nightmare, and nothing could be further from the truth. "Riley, the reason I don't want to sleep with you isn't that I'm afraid of your nightmares. It's because I'm afraid if I lose any more of my heart to you, I won't be able to recover, and you don't seem willing to come home and work things out. But, either way, I'm here, just down the hall. Sweet dreams Riley". She walked into the room they had shared the night before and closed the door.

Riley had some serious thinking to do. He stared at that closed door for long minutes. Was it possible that Hannah and even more importantly Maddie could be okay with the fact that he might have a nightmare at times? Was it really keeping them safe if he exposed them to his trauma and PTSD? Would being with Hannah help him get past his PTSD? So many things that he didn't know the answers to. The one thing he did know what that he loved Hannah and Maddie. But was love enough to get them through his tormented nights and could they come out stronger and more in love on the other side. He wasn't going to get any answers standing here staring at her closed bedroom door, so he walked down the hall to one of the smaller bedrooms, it had actually been the one that he had slept in most often when his family stayed here when he was a kid. Sleep didn't come easy his mind was just too consumed with all that he had to process. In the end though, he realized that there was only one decision to be made. Unless he wanted to spend the rest of his life holed up in this cabin and never go back to his home and family, he had to go back. As far as Hannah and Maddie, the time had come for BACA to take a step back. The man was in prison, there had been no attempts by any of his friends or relatives to cause any trouble, so their presence wasn't needed. They would still be there, in the background and on call if they were ever needed again, but for now, the close cover was over. Maybe that would end up being a good thing. Riley and Hannah could date, but he would sleep alone in his own home in his own bed. He could gage his nightmares to see if his theory was right, did Hannah's 'sweet dreams' wish actually help him or was that all in his own head? When he fell asleep, he was no closer to knowing what the best thing was to do than he had been when he left Hannah's house after his nightmare.

Chapter Sixteen

Hannah woke before Riley did so she quietly made her way out to the porch they often sat on. She turned her chair so that she would be able to see if Riley came out the door. She wanted to make a phone call, but she wanted to be careful just how much he heard of her conversation.

When Sophie answered, Hannah said "Good Morning, Sophie. How are things going with Maddie? I hope she's not giving you any trouble."

"No, not at all, we love having her here." Sophie said. "How's Riley doing?"

"I don't know." Hannah said with a deep sigh. "He's just so certain that he scared Maddie and I when he had the nightmare. I have tried to tell him we were startled but not afraid of him. How could we ever be afraid of him, he's been the one that protected us. He would never hurt us. We all know that, but he doesn't seem so certain that we can get past that."

"Well, I don't know everything that happened to him over there. I know parts of it, but I don't think nightmares would be uncommon for anyone that lived through any of that." Sophie said.

"I agree, but I don't know if I can convince him that it's okay even if he does have them." Hannah said. "Sophie, I love him, and I want to be with him, but if he can't do that, then is it fair for me to try to push him?"

Sophie didn't answer right away, but when she did, she had words of wisdom for Hannah. "Look, I am one of those types of people that believe that if you love something, you have to set it free, if it comes back, it's yours, if it doesn't, it never was. Now, that's not saying that you just walk away because Riley is being stubborn right now, but you can only offer him your love and acceptance, if he isn't going to take it, then you have to take care of you and Maddie and let Riley figure things out for himself."

"Thanks, Sophie." Hannah said. "I'll let you know when I'm headed back. Thanks for keeping Maddie for me."

"It's no problem, we'll see you soon." Sophie said and then hung up.

Hannah sat there for a long time mulling over Sophie's words, but in the end, she made the only decision she could make. She went into the cabin and started a pot of coffee and began cooking breakfast.

When Riley walked into the room, she greeted him warmly and walked over and kissed him briefly. "Good morning, Riley. Breakfast is almost ready. Coffee is finished if you want some."

Riley grabbed a cup of coffee and sat at the table. The plates and silverware had already been set so he took his place. "I would have been glad to help, you should have woken me up."

"It's no problem, I haven't really cooked in a few days, I figured it was my turn." Hannah finished up the eggs and bacon and placed them on the table then she grabbed the toast and sat across from Riley.

They both ate in silence for a bit, then Hannah asked, "How did you sleep?"

Riley was pretty sure she was asking about nightmares, although she most likely would have heard it if he had had one. "It took me a while to fall asleep. I've got a lot on my mind I guess." he admitted softly.

"I know, and I do too, but I realized something this morning and I need to tell you what I've decided.

Riley didn't like the sound of that, but he nodded for her to continue.

"Riley, I love you, or I'm in love with you or however you want to put it. But Sophie said something this morning when I called to check in on Maddie. She reminded me of an old saying that I used to hear all the time, but I guess I kind of forgot about it." Hannah stated. "The saying is 'if you love something, set it free, if it comes back, it's yours, if it doesn't, it never was'"

Riley looked into her eyes, was she saying that she was leaving, he was pretty sure that was what she was saying.

Hannah continued on "So, I love you and I think I will for a long time to come, but I have to set you free to do whatever you feel is best for you. I came here to tell you that Maddie and I both love you and want you back. I've done that, but I can't make you come home until or unless you are ready to."

Riley just stared at her because he wasn't sure what to say. He had his own demons to exercise, and she was right, only he could decide to hold onto her love and acceptance or let her walk away. He just wasn't sure the demons would go away.

"I'm going to head back home today. Sophie and Bryan have been great with Maddie, but it's time I was there to take care of her myself. I'll still keep my promise to wish you sweet dreams every night until you don't want me to anymore." Hannah took a deep breath and added "I'll tell Maddie that I tried, but you just aren't ready to come home yet." Tears were slowly trailing down her cheeks.

Riley wanted to get up and comfort her. He wanted to tell her that he would be right behind her, but he still wasn't sure that was the best thing for all of them. Until he could sort it all out in his own head, he didn't want to be a burden to anyone else. "I'll let you wish me sweet dreams for the rest of my life, Hannah. I love you too, I just can't be the one to terrorize you or Maddie more than you already have been."

Hannah stood up, she couldn't take anymore, she had already packed her suitcase, so she went and got it and walked out to her car. Riley stood in the doorway and watched her leave. He watched long after he couldn't see the car anymore before he went back and cleaned up the breakfast dishes. Hannah hadn't been able to eat much and that was totally his fault too. A part of him was sure she was better off without him, but most of him wasn't sure that he could live without her. It would be selfish of him to expect her to stay with him though, she had a daughter to consider and no matter how much she loved him, she would always love her daughter more. And that was as it should be.

After he cleaned up the kitchen, Riley went and sat out on the porch. He lost track of the time. He was sure he had been out here for hours because the sun had gone across the sky while he tried to sort out his head. He wanted to call Hannah, but he didn't, he wanted to call Bryan, but he didn't. What could he say to any of them, they knew he was messed up. They couldn't fix him, and he didn't know if he could fix himself. He stayed on that porch until his phone rang. It was dark outside. He looked at the caller ID on his cell. It was

Hannah. He stood up and walked into the cabin as he slid the bar to answer the phone. He headed down the hall to the bedroom he and Hannah had shared the night before as he said, "Hello Hannah."

"Hi Riley." Hannah said, he could hear the sadness in her voice, and he knew he had put it there. "I wasn't sure how late you were going to stay up, but I just tucked Maddie in and I'm getting ready to go to bed soon, so I wanted to call."

"I'm glad you did." Riley said. He laid on the bed and he could smell Hannah on the pillow. He turned his head so that he could inhale her scent while he listened to her voice.

"Anyway, like I said, I'm getting ready for bed, so I wanted to call and tell you good night and sweet dreams, Riley." Hannah said softly.

"Good night and sweet dreams to you too Hannah." Riley said softly. He didn't know what else to say.

"Thank you, Riley. I'll talk to you soon." Hannah said.

Just before she could hang up, Riley said "Hannah?"

"Yes?" she answered.

"Please don't give up on me, I'm trying to sort this all out."

"I'm not going anywhere Riley. I'm right here when you're ready." Hannah stated.

"Good night, Hannah." Riley said softly, and then the phone went silent. He buried his face in the pillow Hannah had used and inhaled her scent until he fell asleep.

****

Hannah had known that sleep wasn't going to come easy to her no matter where she was so when Bryan and Sophie had offered for her and Maddie to stay with them for a couple of days, she readily agreed. She had crawled into the big comfortable bed in the room next to the one Maddie had already claimed as her own and called Riley. It was hard hearing his voice not knowing if he was ever going to come back to her or not, but she had made a promise and she intended to keep it. She wished him sweet dreams and when he had asked her not to give up on him, her heart cracked even more than it already had. When she hung up, she cried into her pillow, trying not to let Maddie hear her. The little girl had done enough crying of her own when she realized that Riley hadn't come with Hannah. Hannah had tried to explain that Riley just wasn't' ready to come home yet but hopefully he would be ready soon. Hannah wasn't going to promise her daughter that he would be home at any time soon because she wasn't sure if that would be true.

Every night she called him and wished him sweet dreams and every night she silently cried herself to sleep. She had called in sick to work, heartbreak was just as bad as any cold could be. She wasn't sleeping well, and she often had a headache because of all of the crying.

Chapter Seventeen

It had been three days since Hannah had left the cabin and as she had promised she had called every night and wished him sweet dreams. It kept the nightmares away, but he still wasn't sleeping well. He went to bed late, really late and it was often mid-morning before he woke up. This morning he woke up to hearing someone yell his name.

"Riley, get your ass out here, you got shit to deal with!" Trevor bellowed from the front door.

Riley didn't bother getting dressed, he was in his boxer briefs, but this was his brother, so it wouldn't be a problem. "What the hell, Trevor?" he asked with a scowl.

"You need to get your ass back home, it's your job to take care of Hannah and Maddie, and any shit that goes down with them related to the jackass that hurt Maddie." Trevor explained.

"I thought he was sentenced and in prison, what happened?" Riley had gone back into the bedroom and grabbed his clothes. He was getting dressed as fast as he could, if something had happened to Hannah or Maddie, he wouldn't be able to live with himself.

"Well, he is but apparently, he has friends in low places. I drove by her house this morning just to make sure things were okay, and I found this." He held up his phone to show Riley pictures of

Hannah's house. There were large letters spray painted all over the front of the house. One side of the front door said 'I'm gonna get you bitch!!!' The other had the words 'slut' and 'whore' in bright red paint.

Riley felt sick to his stomach, here he had been wallowing in self-pity or whatever you wanted to call it and Hannah's house had been vandalized. "Oh, god, what did she say when you talked to her?"

"I didn't talk to her, she's not home. I did forward the pictures on to Bryan though because she's been at his house since she got back from the cabin. He's not going to let her go near the house, but you need to come home and help me figure out who did this, and you need to take care of your girl." Trevor demanded.

"Thank god she's not home." Riley stated. "We need to find out who did this. Did you turn in a report to the police?"

"No, I hauled ass up here. They're going to want a statement from Hannah, and I think you need to be there when she sees the house and when she makes the report." Trevor said. "Unless you've decided that you're done with her in which case, Bryan, Sophie and I will help her figure this out."

"Hell no! I'm not done with her; I just had some stuff to sort out." Riley argued.

"Well, now she's got stuff to sort out and you can either be her boyfriend and help her or, you can walk away now, but make it a clean break, don't contact her again." Trevor ordered.

Not talk to her again, no, that wouldn't happen. Her phone calls every night had been the only thing that kept him from going into a deep dark hole that he might never come out of. She was keeping her promise to call him every night. She was taking care of him even though he didn't deserve it. It was time he got his head out of his ass and went and took care of her. "Let me pack my bags" Riley said. "It'll just be a minute." The military had taught them all to pack light if you could and keep everything neat in case you needed to bug out on a moment's notice. His stuff was in one of two bags, the duffle with his clean clothes and the sack with his laundry. He threw everything together and was following Trevor out the door moments later.

When they got on their bikes, Trevor offered one word of caution. "I know right now you want to get there as fast as possible, but wrecking won't help anyone. Let me take the lead, you follow so I can pace it. I don't need another brother in the hospital holding on to his life by a thread."

Riley didn't like it, but he nodded his agreement. None of them would forget almost losing Bryan to a gunshot wound not that many months ago. As much as he hated to admit it, he would probably speed and be reckless in his attempt to get to Hannah. "Drive by her house on the way to Bryan's. I want to see it for my own eyes. Maybe we can find a hint somewhere about who did it." Trevor agreed and they took off for home.

When they pulled into Hannah's driveway, Riley felt sick to his stomach. Seeing the pictures had been awful, seeing the real thing was disturbing. Knowing that Hannah could have easily been home when this had happened, and the person may not have stopped at just vandalizing her home if Hannah had caught them in the act. He and Trevor walked around the yard, trying to find any kind of a clue. They wouldn't touch anything, and they knew how to search without disturbing any of it. They wanted the police to see the yard in its current state.

Riley motioned Trevor over. "Look, there's a cigarette butt, I don't think that was there the last time Hannah was home."

Trevor knelt down closer to Riley to get a better look. "Is that lipstick on it?" He squinted trying to get a better look. He wanted to pick it up, but he wouldn't.

"Maybe" Riley said trying to lean in for a closer look.

"I saw some footprints over there." Trevor said pointing. "It was a small tennis shoe, like a woman's size, but I assumed it was Hannah's, this makes me think that it's not."

They looked around a little more and both agreed that the evidence all seemed like it was a woman who had done this or at least a woman had been there at some point. "Did he have any sisters or girlfriends or anything?" Riley asked.

"No sisters, and no girlfriends that showed up with him anywhere while I was tracking him. He didn't go to any woman's house or anything like that and as far as we know he had no visitors in jail." Trevor stated.

"Well, it could still be a man and the woman just came along to help." Riley said. "Either way, we need to break this to Hannah and call the police." Riley texted Bryan that they were on their way to tell Hannah about the vandalism. Fortunately, Maddie would be at school.

They rode out to Bryan's house and when Riley walked in, he couldn't help but want to wrap Hannah in his arms and never let her go. He felt at least partially responsible for what had happened to her house. It would clean up and could easily be painted over but having to see it was still going to be hard for her. If he could do this without her ever having to know, he would, but that wasn't an option. As the property owner, she would have to talk to the police.

"Riley, you're back!" she said rushing to him. She paused for a minute though because she wasn't fully sure why he was here, but he didn't look happy.

Riley opened his arms and Hannah stepped into him. He held her for a long time. He wasn't exactly sure where their relationship stood, but he knew that he would be here to protect her until they figured out who was trying to terrorize her. "Hey Hannah, can we talk for a minute in private?" he asked as he pushed her away slightly so that he could look at her face. God she was the most beautiful woman he had ever seen, and he was about to tell her something that would rock her world in a horrible way.

Hannah nodded; she was filled with trepidation at what Riley was going to tell her. Was he breaking it off completely? They walked into what Hannah had come to know was Sophie's workspace/office.

"Sweetheart, I have something to tell you and you're not going to like it." Riley began. He could tell she was dreading whatever it was he had to tell her, but it wasn't going to be what she was probably thinking it was. "While we've been away, someone vandalized your house." At her gasp, he continued. "Nothing is broken as far as I can tell, but they spray painted some nasty comments on the walls. It will be easy to clean up once the police get a look at it. But you have to be the one that reports it to them. I'll give you a ride over there and then we can call it in. Bryan and Sophie will pick up Maddie and stay with her until we get this taken care of."

Hannah didn't know if she should be relieved that he wasn't ending things with her or if she should be upset that someone had done something to her house. For now, she was going to let Riley stand beside her and help her through whatever it was that had happened and when this was over, she would see where their relationship stood. She hoped that the fact that he wanted to stand with her on this meant that he had worked out whatever it was that was holding him back. She knew that he thought they couldn't deal with his nightmares even though she had assured him that they could. But until he was ready there wasn't much else, she could do to try to keep him.

Riley rode slowly to Hannah's house, he wanted to relish the feeling of having her behind him. It had been too long since he had her there. On the ride from the cabin to Hannah's house, he had finally realized the one thing that he should have known all along. People in love worked things out. It was something he had seen in his parents and with Pops and his wife. It wasn't that neither couple had ever faced any struggles, it was that they faced them together. He had been a fool to not come to that conclusion earlier. It took something bad happening to Hannah and his need to help fix it that finally made it click in his mind that she felt the same way. Something bad happened to him and caused his nightmares and he hadn't been willing to let her help him get past them. That was going to change, he was going to open his heart and stop letting his head keep him from happiness. He knew they still had to protect Maddie if he had bad dreams, but they would figure that out together too.

When they pulled up to Hannah's house, Riley felt the sharp intake of breath when she saw what had happened to her house. He wrapped his arms around her as soon as they were both off of the motorcycle. He held her tight and reassured her, "We won't let anything happen to you or Maddie, Hannah. I want you to stay with me or continue to stay with Bryan until we get his all cleaned up and find out who did it."

Hannah just stood there trembling in Riley's arms. Why would anyone do this to her, she had never been mean to anyone and other than seeking justice for her daughter she had always just kept to herself. All she could say is "Why?"

"I don't know, sweetheart, but we'll figure it out together. We can tell Maddie whatever you want her to be told." Riley said. "I would prefer it if you would come and stay at my house, but if you aren't comfortable with that, I am sure Bryan will understand why I want to stay at his place with the two of you."

By that time, a police car was pulling up. Apparently, Trevor had called them when they had arrived at the house. Two officers got out of the car and walked toward Riley and Hannah. Trevor stayed off to the side by his motorcycle, there really wasn't much he could tell them about the graffiti, but he would tell them anything that he knew from his surveillance of her home while BACA had been guarding her.

It was pretty obvious when the officers saw the words on Hannah's house, they both blanched in response. They started in on the usual questions, did she have any idea who did it, was there a past lover that might have felt scorned, things like that. Riley stopped that line of questioning by stating. "I'm a member of BACA and Hannah and her daughter were under my care while the court proceedings were going on. The man who assaulted her daughter was sentenced to prison last Friday. We haven't been here in a few days, this happened while we were away." Riley didn't care what they read into that statement. They had no business knowing if he and Hannah were in a relationship or not. It was their job to figure who had vandalized the house and why and to treat them accordingly. "My brother Trevor was actually the first one to see the damage and he contacted me. He might be your best source of information. We own a PI business, and we didn't touch anything, but we did look around and my brother has some theories. If you need to get into the house, here's the key. He handed over the key to Hannah's house and again, if they read anything into that, he didn't give a damn.

Trevor had stepped up and was showing the officers what they had found, including the cigarette butts and small footprints.

"What did you and Trevor find, do you have an idea who did this?" Hannah demanded.

Riley pulled her tightly to himself again and softly said, "We don't know anything for sure sweetheart, we are sure there was a woman here, from the things we saw but we don't know if she did this or if she was just here with whoever did."

"Why would any woman say such horrible things about me? I don't know any women that I have hurt like that." Hannah said. Riley could hear the fear and uncertainty in her voice and feel the wetness slowly leaking from her eyes onto his chest.

"Hannah" he pulled her away ever so slightly so that he could look her in the eyes, "You most likely don't even know her. If she was acting alone, she was probably his girlfriend or at least she thought she was. I'm sure you've seen those stories on TV about women who fall in love, or at least think they do with some criminal and they write to him in prison and think he's going to love them too. She blames you for what is happening to him, even though there is no way you are to blame. He put himself in this position and she will never understand that."

Trevor walked over to them and said "Thankfully, whoever did this did not gain access to the house." He looked at Riley and added. "I didn't tell them how many hours it had been since I first found this. I'm not sure they would have been happy that I took the ride up to the cabin to get you and bring you back. For the record, I was driving by oh," he pretended to look at his watch and said, "about an hour ago and when I saw it, I contacted you and had you get Hannah here so she could file the report."

"You drove all the way up to the cabin to get him so he could be here for me?" Hannah asked quietly. She wasn't going to give away anything to the police.

Trevor whispered through clenched teeth, "Well, when your brother is being an idiot and hiding from people and trying to handle it all by himself, you do what you have to do to get him to listen."

Riley knew his brother was absolutely right, he had been an idiot and he was hiding from the people who loved him the most when he should have been here at home asking them to help him get past this thing. "I know that, now. I shouldn't have left. But I am here now and I'm going to make sure nothing more happens to you or Maddie." he vowed. "I'll be right back." He walked over to the officer and said "If you don't need us anymore, I'd like to take Hannah out of here. Seeing this hasn't been easy for her."

"We're done with you guys for now, but we need her phone number so we can get in touch if needed." one of the officers said.

Riley pulled out his wallet and handed them a business card.

"Your part of the Triskelion PI company?" the other officer asked.

"I am, and so is my brother." He pointed to Trevor.

"So, were you here strictly as a representative of BACA or was there another investigation going on? If there was, we need to know the details so we can rule out anyone you might have been investigating."

"Nope, strictly here for BACA but you can bet were continuing on in our bodyguard capacity until this gets sorted out." Riley stated. "So, you can call me because she'll be with me or one of my brothers until the investigation is done and the house can be cleaned up. I understand we can't do anything until you are done gathering evidence, but I'd appreciate a call when we have the all clear to do clean up."

"Of course." one of the officers said. "And I assume you won't be doing anymore investigating that will hinder what we need to do."

"We won't get in your way." Riley promised. No way was he going to promise not to at least have Trevor work some of his tech magic to see if he picked up anything.

The officer looked toward Hannah and said "Ma'am, you're free to go, but we may be in touch if we have any questions or information."

Hannah nodded as Riley walked back toward her and they all got on the motorcycles and left. When they got to Bryan's house, they filled the others in on what was going on. Trevor was already on his laptop trying to see if he could find out any more information.

"Well, you can stay here as long as you need to." Sophie said. "And when the police give the all clear I'm sure all of the guys will get your house back in shape before Maddie ever has to see it."

"Thank you." Hannah said. Riley could tell that she was still reeling from what she had seen at her house.

"You're welcome to come and stay at my place too. If you want to." Riley offered.

"It's not that I don't want to be at your house, but I think it's easier on Maddie if we just stay here. She considers this an adventure, but if we were to leave here, I think she might wonder why we aren't going home. She doesn't understand it all, but she's a smart little girl and I worry that she'll start to add things up if we can't go home." Hannah stated.

Although Riley was disappointed, he did understand Hannah's reasoning. They had to keep life as normal as possible for Maddie for however long this took.

"Well, this is interesting." Trevor said while staring at his computer. When the others looked at him with curiosity, he continued "A woman named Molly Stewart tried to visit the jail to see our guy, but I don't find any connection between them before that. There's nothing on his social media that even suggests that he knows who she is. And when she tried to visit, he declined. So, either he doesn't know her, or they aren't getting along anymore."

"How do you know she tried to visit him?" Hannah asked.

"Well, um." Trevor stammered, he wasn't sure just how much Hannah knew and how much Riley wanted her to know.

Riley took the decision out of his brother's hands and stated "Trevor can hack into almost any system around. That's why the Marines recruited him. They got tired of him hacking in to try to find out where Bryan was. So, finding the jail visitation logs is small potatoes for him."

"Wow. Remind me to never get on your bad side." Hannah said with a brief smile, it disappeared when she added, "Not that there's much you could do to ruin my life any more than it already is."

Riley put an arm around her shoulder and drew her close to his side "We're going to fix it all Hannah, this won't last forever. I promise."

Hannah had no more words, she just leaned into Riley and tried to absorb some of his strength.

They spent the rest of the day mostly quiet while Trevor spent most of his time trying to figure out who this woman was and if it were possible that she had been the one to vandalize Hannah's home.

Chapter Eighteen

Riley had asked Hannah if she would mind if he went and picked up Maddie from school. Hannah had been fine with that; she was sure that her daughter would be elated to see Riley was back home. Riley was standing outside the school near his truck so that Maddie wouldn't miss seeing him. She had been getting picked up by Sophie or Bryan most of the time lately. As soon as she saw Riley, she started running full tilt towards him.

"Riley!" she exclaimed as she jumped into his arms "you're home! Are you going to stay at our house now?"

"Actually, Maddie, I think we might all stay at Bryan and Sophie's house for a little while longer if that's okay with you." Riley said carrying her to his truck to help her get in and buckled. "I was hoping you and I could have a little talk on the way though."

"Okay." Maddie said.

When Riley had her secured in her seat he went around to his side and got in. He started the car and backed out of the parking lot. "Maddie. I'm really sorry that I woke you up the other night when I had my bad dream. I didn't mean to scare you."

"I wasn't scared, Riley. I felt bad for you because I've had bad dreams before and I don't like them." she said honestly.

"If I have more bad dreams, will you be scared then?"

"No, if you let me, I'll give you lots of hugs and make the bad dreams go away. That's what my mommy does for me when I have one."

The little girl had so much love and confidence that she could help him with his bad dreams that he was almost convinced that she would be right. Could they become a family, did he dare try with Hannah and see if he could overcome the nightmares?

"Someday soon, I would like to take you to my house. When your mom says it's okay." Riley stated.

"Do you have horses?" Maddie asked.

"No, but I have a big yard and a swimming pool." Riley said.

"Do you have a puppy?" she queried.

"Not yet, but I'm thinking about getting one." Riley offered.

"If you get a puppy, can I come and play with him?" Maddie asked.

"Of course, anytime you mom says you can." Riley said.

They spent the rest of the trip talking about her school day and about where Riley had gone. He told her that maybe sometime they could all go to the cabin so she could see it. By the time they got to Bryan's house, Riley was pretty sure that he knew that he wanted both of them in his life forever. And he trusted that they could work through his nightmares together if he had them. But he also knew that now wasn't the time to bring that up with Hannah. With the damage done to her house, she already had enough on her mind.

Every night, Hannah and Riley tucked Maddie into her bed and every night she prayed for everyone in Riley's family and her own family. This little girl had a heart as big as the universe and loved everyone she knew. When Riley thought about the fact that someone had taken advantage of her love and trust he saw red. And knowing that it was possible that the scum was still trying to reach out from prison to terrorize them even more made him wish the guy would never get out.

After tucking Maddie in, Riley walked Hannah down the hall to her room and kissed her goodnight. He never tried to go any further, he knew it wasn't going to happen with Maddie next door and he had some penance to do for walking out on her the way he had. Oh, she wasn't demanding any, but he knew he had been a jackass when he didn't stay and try to sort it out with her. Every night she wished him sweet dreams and then went into her room and closed the door almost all the way. He wasn't sure if she kept it open in case Maddie needed her or if she did it for him. He was sleeping on the couch every night. It wasn't that his brother didn't have a bedroom he could stay in, but the couch was the closest place to Hannah, and it was between her and anyone that might try to get into the house. Not that anyone would make it with the security system Bryan had, but he wasn't taking any chances with his girls.

Over the course of the next couple of days, Trevor had enough evidence that they were sure his original suspect had been the one to put the graffiti on Hannah's house. What they didn't know was why and without a valid theory, they couldn't exactly walk up to the police station and demand she be arrested. Besides, some of Trevor's methods might lean slightly towards the illegal side. What they had to do was figure out how to get the woman to slip up and get herself caught. The one thing that Trevor knew for sure was that the woman tried to visit him in jail at least once a week and every time he turned her away. Whether that was because he didn't know her, or he wanted nothing more to do with her that might connect him to the crime she committed they weren't sure. Trevor had found the small hardware store where she had bought the paint, but again, without giving away his methods it was hard to know how to get that information to the police.

Bryan and Trevor came up with a plan, but they were pretty sure Riley wasn't going to like it. They wanted to present the idea to Hannah, but they wouldn't do that without Riley being okay with that plan. So, they sat him down and told him their idea. They had been right; he wasn't okay with it. They did however convince him to let Hannah make her own decision.

The following morning after Maddie went to school, they all sat at the table to discuss the idea. Trevor began with the report of what he knew about the woman and his evidence that made it pretty hard to deny she had to have been the one that did it.

"So, here's the idea we have, because it doesn't seem like the cops have a clue yet, and we can't exactly tell the cops what we know because not all of it was found in a way that Trevor can admit to." Bryan began. "We know that she attempts to visit him at least once a week. There are two days that visitation is possible. We want to plant you outside of the jail so that it looks like you are going to see him." At Hannah's immediate shake of her head, Riley squeezed her hand and Bryan held up a finger to ask her to bear with him a little longer. "We don't want you to go anywhere near him or the actual jail. From what we can tell, he never accepts her visits. What we don't know is if that is because he doesn't know her and she's some demented 'fan' if you can call it that or if he's just trying to distance himself from more trouble."

Trevor turned his computer screen towards her and continued with their idea. "This is the entrance that visitors have to use to sign in to see an inmate. I would be sitting on this bench right here" he pointed to a park bench at the side of the walkway. "With high powered recording equipment that will be able to pick up anything she may say to you. We are hoping that she will give away something that will incriminate her in the damage done to your house."

"Won't it look suspicious if you're sitting there with some big old recording device?" Hannah asked.

Trevor pulled a small thing about the size of a pea out of a box and attached it to his phone. "It would if it had to be large, but it doesn't with today's technology this can pick up and amplify voices up to thirty feet away. Since I'll be less than ten it won't be a problem."

"Riley and I will be in our vehicles parked right out here." Bryan continued, pointing to two areas in the parking lot. "If she attempts to come close enough to touch you, it's all off and we step in. We won't let her get a hand on you."

Sophie looked around at the guys and though she knew they could easily handle what they said they would do; she also knew how terrifying something like this would be. "I'd like to walk with her." she began "the woman won't be alerted to me walking with Hannah. I'm just the bestie hanging out. If one of you were to walk with Hannah, the woman won't say anything, but if I'm there, she will feel less threatened, and I think Hannah will feel better if she's not alone."

Bryan almost objected to that plan, but he took a second to sort it out in his head. What Sophie said was right, none of them could be spotted with Hannah or the woman wouldn't do anything. And even though the protector in him didn't want Sophie that close to the situation, he couldn't justify keeping her away when he was asking Riley to send his woman in as bait. He knew that Sophie could take care of herself too. He had taught her some basic self-defense so the only thing he could do was agree. "If Hannah is willing to do this, I'm okay with you going with her."

Hannah really didn't want to do this but having Sophie right beside her would give her more strength to get through it than she had on her own. Sophie had said she trusted these men and that they had protected her from a stalker, so could Hannah really justify not trusting them when they would all be right there, and it was a public place with police officers nearby. In the end, she agreed to do it. The visiting hours were in the evening, so they made arrangements with Summer to come and stay with Maddie that night.

Chapter Nineteen

Trevor had shown them a picture of the woman he was sure had done the vandalism so they would know if she approached them. They were supposed to signal, but they also needed to interact enough to try to get her to say something to incriminate herself. Hannah wasn't sure she would be able to say anything to the woman, but Sophie seemed confident that she could get her to talk. If she was even there. They couldn't initiate conversation because they weren't supposed to know who she was, but they could attempt to get her attention in other ways. The hope was that if she knew where Hannah lived, she would also recognize her if they walked past each other.

As they walked slowly toward the building that housed the local jail, Sophie spotted the woman coming up from the other side of the parking lot. She knew they had to be within a certain range of Trevor for him to be able to record what was going on. He was hoping for video along with the audio so there could be no doubt as to who said what. Sophie gave the signal so the guys would be on alert, and softly said to Hannah "Keep up". She picked up her pace so that they would be near Trevor at the same time that Molly did. Fortunately, Hannah had looked up and seen the reason for the increase in speed too. Although she had paled at the sight of the woman, she did keep in step with Sophie.

When they were within earshot of Molly and Trevor, Sophie said "I can't believe some woman tries to come and see him all the time and he turns her down. You would think she would give up."

Molly looked up and it was obvious that she recognized Hannah. Although they had been able to keep Maddie's name and face out of the papers and the news, a few random photos of Hannah had been posted in papers during the trial. Molly started babbling "What are you doing here, you bitch? You're the reason he's in here! I've loved him for years and he wanted nothing to do with me after he met you and your little brat."

Hannah started to go towards the woman. She could spew whatever vile hatred she wanted to at Hannah, but when she mentioned Maddie, the mama bear was ready to let go and attack the woman. Sophie held her arm to keep her from doing anything stupid. It only took the squeeze from her friend to get her back on track though. "Are you the one that painted those awful words on my house?" That was the one thing they needed to hear from her mouth. If she would answer that one question, Hannah could walk away and never have to see the woman again.

"Yes, it was me, and you deserve so much more. You're the reason he's in jail, You're the reason he doesn't want me." Molly screamed. "I hate you; I wish you were dead. Maybe someday I'll come to your house in the middle of the night and get even with you!" She started to lunge at Hannah, but her yelling had attracted the attention of some of the police officers from inside the building. Two of them took her by the arm to hold her back.

"What's going on here?" one of them asked.

Bryan and Trevor were both there to talk to the officers. "This woman is the one who vandalized a home last weekend. Here's a copy of the complaint number." Trevor said pulling a paper out of his pocket. "As you just witnessed, this woman was also attempting to attack our client."

"And who are you?" the other officer asked.

"We're from Triskelion Private Investigations, we have been guarding this woman both as a client of ours and an assignment through BACA." Bryan stated, showing them his card. He knew that some cops may or may not like working with a PI, but all of them knew who BACA was and would realize that a child had been involved at some point in the case.

"I have a recording of everything that was said prior to you coming out here." Trevor stated.

"And why were you out here recording this?" they asked.

"We can explain and answer all of those questions, but as you can see, Hannah has been traumatized by this woman's outburst. Would you allow our brother to take her out of here for now? If you need to talk to her, we would be glad to set up a time when she isn't so distressed." Bryan stated. He pretty much sounded like they really needed to agree, or they weren't going to like the next steps he would take. Bryan wouldn't hesitate to get the attorneys from Five Sloths involved if he needed to. "And you will see that a petition for an Order of Protection was filed on Hannah's behalf a few days ago."

Hannah was just about ready to drop. She had been shaking so hard and she couldn't see straight. Her knees began to buckle, and strong arms wrapped around her. Riley was there and she didn't have to worry any more. He cradled her to him and held her until the police officers said she could go for now. But they would be in touch if they needed anything more from her. Riley walked her to his truck and helped her in. He knew his brothers and Sophie would take care of the rest.

When they were pulling out of the parking lot, Riley said "Hannah, I don't want to take you home until you have a chance to process all of this and calm down. Maddie will sense something if you are too upset. Would it be okay if we just drove for a while?"

Hannah simply nodded; she didn't even have words right now.

Riley just drove around with no particular destination in mind. He kept encouraging Hannah by saying this like "You kept it together really well back there Hannah." Or "If you need to talk, I'm here to listen."

Finally, after they had been driving for a good half hour, Hannah softly said "I have a restraining order against her? How do I have that?"

"Well, we wanted to cover our bases just in case, so one of the Five Sloth guys got it set up. We didn't want her to be able to get too close to you and we hoped it would keep her off your property too. We weren't sure if she would try to go back." Riley explained.

Another long time passed before Hannah said "How can someone be so hateful to someone they don't even know? I've never done anything to that woman and yet she hates me so much."

"Well, she's obviously obsessed with him and is delusional about what you mean to him." Riley said. "It's nothing you did sweetheart. Some people just can't comprehend the real world."

"Will I have to go to court over this or testify against her?" Hannah asked.

"I don't know, I'm sure you'll probably have to make a statement at some point, but we'll face whatever needs to be done together." Riley assured. "Look, Hannah, I owe you an apology. I never should have left that night. I know that now. I should have stayed with you and Maddie and talked it out. I realize that we were starting a relationship and I should have at least given you the chance to tell me if you could live with my nightmares or not. I don't know when or if I'll have them, but I shouldn't have just assumed that you wouldn't want to be around me because of them. I would really like to move forward with you and see where things might go." He paused and then said "I'd like for you and Maddie to move in with me. Even if you aren't ready to sleep with me. After what has happened to you two, I don't think I can feel like you're safe in your house anymore and I don't fit on your couch all that well. We can do whatever you want to my house, we can get one of those play structure things if you think Maddie would like it. She told me she wants a puppy, and I am totally up for that, if and when you think the time is right. If the only way you can move in with me is as a friend and someone I want to protect, I'll be okay with that. It won't mean that I won't try to convince you to fall in love with me. But I'll respect whatever decision you make. If sleeping on your couch is all I can have, then I'll take it."

"Riley, pull over." Hannah demanded.

He pulled to the side of the road and looked at Hannah.

She scooted closer to him and said, "Riley, I never stopped loving you. I just wanted you to let me in and let me be a part of whatever you need. You've been protecting Maddie and I from the big bad wolf for weeks now. I just want you to let me help you face whatever bothers or scares you too." She leaned into him and kissed him. "I love you Riley Lawson, I have for a long time, and a nightmare isn't going to scare me away. The only thing that will make me go away is if you push me out of your life."

Riley pulled her to him as much as the steering wheel would allow and held her tight. "Hannah, I've always been the little brother and always had people taking care of me. I know it's not necessarily what I should have done, but once I joined the Green Beret, I told myself that I needed to man up and take care of others instead of them taking care of me. I haven't ever relied on anyone since that day. I am close to my family, but I was determined to take care of things for myself. I didn't think about the fact that it's supposed to be different when you are in a relationship like what I was hoping to have with you. I felt like my nightmares were a weakness that I needed to hide from anyone until I could make them go away. I'm sorry that I didn't let you in. It wasn't my intention to push you away. I just didn't want you to have to deal with my crap on top of everything else you were going through."

"But if we are going to have a real relationship, it's our crap, not just yours. We share our highs and our lows, Riley. That's the only way it works." Hannah said not letting him go.

"I understand that now, and I do what a real relationship with you Hannah. I know that we have to be careful about Maddie and not let her jump to any conclusions about where we are at. I don't want to confuse her with things. She told me the kids at school asked her if I was her new daddy. She told them I was her friend. So, I know we have to be cautious about how we are, but I want to be with you. I want more of what we have had." He kissed her deeply.

She pressed herself against him and said "I want that too Riley. We will just take things one day at a time and we'll talk to Maddie if she has questions. I am not sure about moving in with you, I will have to see what she thinks of that too. That small house is all she knows, she's lived there her whole life, and with all of the upheaval of life lately, I don't want to push her into more than she's ready for."

"I get that, and like I said, if all I can have for now is the couch, I'll take it." Riley promised.

Hannah pulled away a little and said, "We should get back, Sophie and Bryan will wonder where we are if they get there before we do."

"Right." Riley agreed turning back to the steering wheel. He drove them back to Sophie and Bryan's house.

It wasn't late, so Maddie was still up waiting for them. "Did you have fun, mommy?" she asked innocently.

Hannah wasn't sure how to respond to that, but Riley stepped in, and he sat on the couch and patted his lap for Maddie to sit if she wanted to. She climbed up and he told her "Sometimes adults have to take care of business. It's not always fun, but it needs to be done. We had some business to take care of tonight, but we got it settled for now."

"Like when mommy sits at the table and pays the bills." Maddie said.

"Right, exactly like that." Riley agreed. "We don't have fun paying bills, but we have to do it, or things don't get taken care of."

"Okay, I'm glad you got it all taken care of then, I missed you." Maddie said giving him a big hug. Hannah had sat beside Riley on the couch and Maddie looked at her "I missed you too mommy. Are we going to stay here or go home?"

Hannah was a little hesitant to give a direct answer to that, she knew they were staying for at least tonight, but they had been told that they couldn't clean up the house until the police were done with the investigation. Now that the woman had basically confessed, she wasn't sure if they were going to be able to clean up the graffiti sooner rather than later. "We're staying here for at least another night, it's getting close to bedtime, but I'm not sure how much longer we're going to be here." Hannah explained. "Why, are you wanting to go home?"

"Not really. I didn't bring all of my toys, so I kind of miss some of them, but being here is fun too." Maddie said. Semper Fi chose that exact moment to jump into Riley's lap and lick Maddie in the face the little girl began to giggle.

"See, Semper Fi would miss you if you left right now." Summer said. Maddie got off of Riley's lap so the puppy would chase her around the house. Summer asked, "how'd it go?"

"Well, successful I guess if you consider being berated by a crazy lady success." Hannah said. She looked at Maddie to be sure she was still completely engrossed with the puppy.

Summer spoke in a quiet voice just in case Maddie was listening. "Did Trevor get what he needed?"

"Pretty sure he did. As soon as a couple of cops came out to assess the situation, I got Hannah out of there as soon as I could" Riley said. "Bryan, Sophie and Trevor are giving statements and Hannah and I will probably have to go in at some point to give ours, but they were okay with her getting out of there once they saw what the commotion was doing to Hannah."

"Well, I hope they take care of her." Summer said, weighing her words because of the child in the room. What she implied with her look was that she hoped the woman got locked up for a long time.

"I think they'll do a psych eval for sure." Riley said. "She seemed a little off her rocker to me."

"Trevor never found any connection with them?" Summer asked.

"Not anything recent, there's no telling if they knew each other years ago or if she's just fixated on him now for some reason." Riley said.

Hannah looked a little uncomfortable with the topic, Riley wasn't sure if it was the fact that Maddie wasn't far away or if she was still spooked by it all. He looked at Summer and gave a slight slash of his hand letting her know the topic was closed for now. She gave a small dip of her head to acknowledge that she understood. "Well, I should head out." Summer said. "If you ever need me to watch Maddie again, just let me know. We had a lot of fun."

"Maddie, come say goodbye to Summer." Hannah said.

Maddie ran over and hugged Summer around the legs. "Thank you for coming to play with me Aunt Summer."

Hannah looked a little puzzled at the title added to the name. Summer just shrugged like she had no idea where that came from. When Maddie was done with the hug, Riley walked his sister to the door.

"I don't know when they're going to clear us to do clean up on the house, but as soon as they do, I want to get a crew in there fast to clean up and repaint the whole thing, maybe even a new color if Hannah wants that. I don't want there to be any traces visible at all." Riley said.

"Let me know, I'm sure Jeremy and the Five Sloth guys would be willing to help if they can." Summer said.

"I will, thanks." Riley said. "Summer, I know when I first came home, I shut all of you out and wouldn't tell you what happened to me over there. Sometime soon, I'd like to tell you about it. I realize now that shutting down and keeping everyone out of it wasn't best for them or for me and I'd like to change that."

Summer wrapped her arm around his neck and said "We all knew something happened, more than just the shrapnel wound. I think Bryan may have checked into it a little more than we think he did, but I'd be glad to listen anytime you want to tell the story, Rye." She kissed him on the cheek and walked out to her SUV.

By the time Sophie and Bryan got home, Maddie had been tucked into bed, she had school the next morning. So, the adults sat down to talk about what had happened after Riley and Hannah had left.

"Well, with all of the evidence we had and our statements, there really isn't much more that needs to be done." Bryan began. "They do want Hannah to come down sometime in the next day or two to give a statement. It's not much of a statement since she doesn't know the woman and has no clue why she defaced the house. They'll ask her about all of that, but she won't have any answers to give them."

"Does anyone have a clue why she did this?" Hannah asked.

"Well, best we can figure from what Trevor put together and what she told the cops, she's basically delusional and thinks this guy is her soulmate or something like that. We don't think she even knew him before his original arrest when Maddie's case started. She saw him in the papers, and I don't fully understand any of it, but then again, I never understand these women who fall for inmates, and since then she has followed his case and basically stalked the guy. When he was found guilty and went to jail, she decided that Hannah was coming between her and her true love." Bryan explained.

Hannah just sat shaking her head for a long while.

"Well, in a sense, it's like what happened to me," Sophie began. "Even though my ex was an abusive asshole that ran after the cops were called on him, he decided that he wanted me back and he stalked me. I think it's got to be a mental break of some sort. I mean who feels that way about someone they haven't even met. With my ex at least he knew how awesome I really was." She was smiling, trying to make things a little lighter.

"Yes" Bryan said, "He realized too late that you were awesome and that's a good thing for me." He leaned over and kissed her briefly. "Rye, can I talk to you for a minute in my office. We need to make sure we all have the same story to cover Trevor's snooping skills as usual."

"Sure." Riley stood and told Hannah "I shouldn't be long but if you need to get to bed, I understand."

"Nope, I'm good. I'm still on my leave of absence from work and I don't think I'd sleep well right now anyway, maybe Sophie and I can have a cup of tea and chat." She said, looking hopefully at her friend.

"Sure, I'm not going anywhere until Bryan is done anyway." Sophie said getting up to put water in the tea kettle.

"Can I ask you something?" Hannah asked after the men were behind the closed door of Bryan's office.

"Sure, anything." Sophie said. She got out the cups and tea assortment and put them on the table then sat to talk with Hannah until the water was heated.

"I know you don't have kids, but I was raised really old fashioned. Do you think it's wrong for Riley and I to be open about our relationship with Maddie, or do you think it will confuse her?" Hannah asked.

"Well, I think that depends. If you and Riley aren't really sure you're planning to be a long-term thing, and I don't necessarily mean marriage at this point, then no, I think it's best to not let Maddie think that Riley is going to be around for a while. But, if there's any chance that you can be long term, then Maddie would understand. She's almost nine. I think if you sit her down and tell her that you and Riley are dating or boyfriend and girlfriend or however you want to say it, she'll understand. I know she loves Riley already and I know he loves her just as much." Sophie assured. She got up and grabbed the tea kettle and brought it to the table. "If you and Riley don't work out, I don't think it's going to make much difference to Maddie at this point if you were in a relationship or not, she's going to miss Riley either way."

"I know, and I do want a long term relationship with Riley." Hannah began. "He told me tonight that he would like me to think about moving in with him at some point."

"And how do you feel about that?" Sophie asked.

"I think I would like it very much, but I don't want to do it if it's the wrong thing for Maddie." Hannah said.

"Well, you can always ask her, be honest and completely up front. Tell her that you aren't marrying Riley, but you are thinking about staying at his house for a while to see if maybe you can be a good couple. Give her the benefit of the doubt. She's a very smart little girl. I think she's already kind of thinking there's something between you two." Sophie stated.

"I am wondering if she does, tonight she called Summer 'Aunt Summer'. I'm not sure it that's one of those things that kids do, where people seem like family even though they really aren't or if she's actually thinking that Summer might be her aunt at some point in the future."

"Well, kids often see a lot more than we give them credit for. So, who knows." Sophie shrugged. "But I don't think you can go wrong by having an open and honest conversation with her. Explain that you and Riley like each other and want to see if you make a good couple. And be open to her asking questions if she has them. Honesty is always the best policy."

They drank their tea and chatted about their evening and what had happened with Molly. "There's a part of me that wants her to be punished, but there's also a part of me that hopes she gets help if it is some kind of mental breakdown." Hannah said.

"I agree with you, Sweetheart." Riley said coming back from Bryan's office. "Are you ready for bed, you had a long and stressful day."

"I am." Hannah said standing up. "Thanks for the tea and conversation Sophie. I appreciate you letting us stay here and being such a good friend to me."

Riley walked Hannah down the hall to her room and was ready to give her a kiss goodnight and head for the couch he had been sleeping on, but Hannah asked him if he would come in and just hold her for a while. "Gladly sweetheart, I'll stay as long as you want me to." Riley agreed.

Hannah went into the bathroom attached to her bedroom and put her pajamas on while Riley took off his boots pulled back the covers and got comfortable on the bed. When Hannah came out, she was in simple short pjs, but she still looked beautiful to Riley. She cuddled up beside him and laid her head on his chest.

"You go ahead and sleep if you can Hannah, I'm right here to hold you and since I'm fully dressed, even if Maddie did walk in, we can easily explain that you fell asleep while we were talking." Riley assured. "I just need to know if you want me to leave when you fall asleep or if you want me to stay."

"Stay please." Hannah said. "I'm exhausted, but I don't know if I will sleep well or not after what has happened. I'd like to have you near me."

"Then that's what I'll do." Riley said.

"In case we both fall asleep, sweet dreams, Riley." She sounded sleepy already.

"You too, Hannah. Sweet dreams." He kissed her on the forehead and held her tight to him.

Chapter Twenty

It had been a week since the incident at the jail. Riley and Hannah had gone in and given their statements, although neither one of them really had much information to give the police. They didn't know the woman and they didn't know why she had fixated on Hannah. A few days after their statements had been given, Bryan got the all clear to go ahead and clean up Hannah's house. Riley told Hannah that the house would be ready for them by Monday if she wanted to return. She hadn't looked overly thrilled with that idea but had acknowledged what he had told her.

The following Monday, Riley had taken Hannah to work and would pick her up so that they could go to her house. It hadn't been decided yet what they were going to tell Maddie about when they were going home. Since she didn't know the real reason, they had stayed away, they were going to have to break it to her that it was time to go home.

When Riley pulled into Hannah's driveway, he immediately sensed her change in mood. He got out of the truck and walked around to her side of the vehicle. He put his arm around her, and they slowly walked to the house. Hannah seemed to be very hesitant to get closer. Riley didn't push her to go any faster than she was ready to go.

Hannah felt like she had cement blocks for feet. Her brain told her that the house had been cleaned up. It didn't look like it had the last time she had seen it, but that didn't mean that she didn't still picture those words on the front of her house. How was she going to face this house everyday seeing those words in her brain? How many days or weeks would it be before she didn't see those bright red letters calling her horrible names? She knew now that the woman had had a psychotic break and was getting treatment. She never had known the man who she had become infatuated with, although she had a history of abuse from a man who had looked similar. So somehow in her brain, she had fixated on him. Hannah couldn't understand that other than to relate it as something similar to Stockholm syndrome where a person became unnaturally attached to their abuser and since her actual abuser was gone, the man who looked like him had gained her infatuation. In her head, it all made sense, well, not really made sense, but she could understand it in a clinical way. But those words on her house didn't make sense in any form. And in her head, they were still there. She didn't realize that she had stopped walking completely until Riley said something.

"Are you okay, sweetheart?"

She looked at Riley rather than looking at the house. "I don't know. Why do I still see those awful words in my head? I can't even look at the house because in my mind I'm sure they are still there even though logically I know that you and your brothers cleaned it up."

If there was one thing Riley understood in life, it was PTSD. "It's kind of normal actually, Hannah. It's a form of PTSD."

"When will it go away?" she asked in a panic. "I can't have this reaction every time I try to walk into my own home."

"There's no way to know how long it will last." Riley said. "It's not something anyone can put a time frame on. If you think counseling will help, I am sure Bryan and Sophie would be glad to have you stay as long as you need to. Or you and Maddie can come and stay with me. If you want to, we can come back here and work on you being able to go in how ever often you want to."

"And what if I can't ever go in there again?" Hannah asked.

"Well, then we deal with that if we need to." Riley said. Hannah hadn't realized it, but he had turned her back toward his truck and had been gently steering her away from the house. "Why don't we go for a drive and talk about it for a while before you decide what you want to do, Hannah. Nothing needs to be figured out today."

Hannah wasn't really paying attention to where they were going, she was going over things in her head, but she did realize that they had pulled into Riley's house. When she looked at him quizzically, he just said "I wanted to show you something, so I figured now was as good a time as any. We don't even have to go inside if you don't want to, it's in the backyard." He took her hand when she got out of the truck and walked her around the house.

When they had gotten through the gate in the fence that enclosed the non-wooded sides of his yard. Hannah looked surprised at what had been added to the yard since she had been here a few weeks before.

"I built it in case" Riley began. "I'm not trying to pressure you to move here, but I've known for a while now that I want you and Maddie in my life long term. I figured I could tell you all day that I want you here, but this was the best way to show you."

Hannah was looking at the largest wooden play structure she had ever seen. There were slides and ladders, swings, and a fort. There was also a large trampoline. "You even got a trampoline?" Hannah asked.

"I did." Riley said, taking her hand and walking toward it. "The best thing about this trampoline is that it's rated for a six hundred and sixty pound weight capacity." He picked her up by the waist and set her on the edge of the trampoline. He leaned down and took off her shoes. He quickly removed his own shoes and joined her on the edge of the trampoline. "Come on, sweetheart, let's jump and play and have fun like we don't have a care in the world." He stood up and tugged her with him. He began a slow bounce until he was sure she was going to be okay with it.

Hannah couldn't believe he had bought a trampoline that would hold a few adults or lots of kids. "Maddie's never really had a place where she could invite many friends. She would be the envy of all the kids if she lived here."

Riley knew they were going to continue that talk at some point later, but for now, he just wanted to let Hannah have fun and not have to think. He grabbed both of her hands and started jumping with more force. Soon they were bouncing like two little kids and Hannah began giggling. "Are you having fun sweetheart?" Riley asked after several minutes of acting like a little kid. He gradually began slowing his bouncing so that they could eventually stop.

"I am, thank you for taking me away from it all for a while Riley." Hannah said. The trampoline was still bouncing, but not so much that she couldn't pull herself closer to Riley. She put her arms around his neck and said, "You're a pretty awesome man, do you know that, Riley Lawson."

Riley leaned down and took Hannah's mouth in a deep kiss. "You're awesome too Hannah. I know that it may not always feel that way to you, but you have put up with so much shit in the last few months, and you're still standing."

"I don't know about that; I can't even walk into my own house right now." she said looking down to her feet.

Riley put his finger under her chin and lifted her face so he could look her in the eyes. "Hannah, that's nothing to feel bad about. You're a great mom, you've kept Maddie from all of this stuff with the graffiti, you stood beside her and believed her when you found out what happened to her. Not all parents do that. You've been a single mom for a long time and Maddie's a pretty amazing kid. You've done a great job raising her, but there's no shame in needing someone to help take care of you for a while. When I came home, my siblings wouldn't let me close in on myself. If I didn't show up at the shop, one of my brothers was banging on my door telling me I had to go to work. I'm pretty sure my sister purposely always made too much food so that she could invite me over. She'd always say that she hadn't realized the recipe would make so much, but I had a hot cooked meal more nights than I would have had on my own. Even Pops, he'd call me and tell me that his coffee machine was making a funny noise and he didn't want to pay a repair man, so he wanted me to come look at it. I had a support system that wouldn't give up. You've got one now too Hannah. Not just me, my family all loves you and we plan to be here for you for the long haul. I admit I'm being totally selfish here, I want you and Maddie to move in with me, even if you and I have to keep it platonic for now. I need you to be here with me so that I know you are both safe, but I also need you here with me because I sleep better when you're close by. Please, Hannah, come and stay with me. You don't even have to go pack your stuff. I'm sure Sophie and Summer would be glad to do it. At least for a little while and then after we see how things go, you can decide if you're ready to go back to that house, or if you want to get rid of it. If it's always going to be a bad memory, you can sell it and even if you don't want to live here forever, you can move somewhere else. Please, Hannah." He looked deep into her eyes trying to will her to choose him.

    Hannah could see the sincerity in Riley's eyes. She had been trying to keep Maddie from being hurt all her life, and yet, she had gotten hurt anyway. She had to admit that no matter how hard you tried, you couldn't always keep your child out of harm's way. She also had to admit that Riley had done everything in his power to protect Maddie too. He hadn't so much as kissed Hannah or held her hand anytime Maddie might be around. He didn't want the little girl to think something was happening if it wasn't. Hannah was pretty sure she and Riley would be a great team for the long term. She knew beyond any doubt that he and his family would be good for Maddie. There was still a part of her that thought she should wait until she was sure it was going to be something real before Maddie got involved. Then again, how was she going to know if it was something real if she didn't step out and try. Maddie was getting old enough that she understood so much more. In a lot of ways, she had been forced to grow up way too fast in the last year. She had done so well when she had to go to court because she knew she had people that loved and supported her and none of them loved her more than Riley did. She knew she was taking a long time to sort it all out in her head and she very much appreciated the fact that he just held her and let her process. He wasn't trying to convince her one way or the other. Finally, she knew that she had to try even if it didn't work out, she had to try. She wouldn't do herself or her daughter any good if she kept everyone at arm's length.

"I'd like to present the idea to Maddie although I can't imagine her not wanting to move here especially when she sees the pool, trampoline and play structure. As far as the sleeping arrangements, I'm not sure yet, I want to see how Maddie takes it all. And of course, the basement needs to be locked, or at least the one room does." Hannah said.

"Done." Riley said, "Anything you need Hannah and anything Maddie needs."

She didn't doubt that he would live up to that promise. "Before we tell Maddie about moving in, I have one request." Hannah said smiling.

"Like I said, anything, sweetheart." Riley stated.

"I'd like for you to make love to me on this trampoline. I don't think we'll get much opportunity once we bring Maddie here." Hannah said stretching up to kiss him.

"That will be my pleasure sweetheart." Riley said pulling her down with him on the trampoline. It wasn't totally dark, but it was dusk. Riley was pretty sure they didn't have to be afraid of having an audience, well other than an animal or two in the woods. He would have to see if Hannah would prefer that there was a fence back there since Maddie would be staying here. But that was a conversation for later Riley thought. When Hannah straddled him and took off her shirt, he changed that to much, much later for that conversation.

****

The following day, Hannah told Maddie that they were going for a ride. She wanted to show Maddie something and they needed to have a long talk. She had decided that she wanted to do the first part without Riley so that Maddie didn't feel any pressure to make a certain decision. Hannah knew Riley wouldn't try to influence her daughter, but Maddie loved Riley so much that she might want to please him whether or not it was truly what she wanted to do.

When they were driving down the road, Hannah began. "So, Maddie I want to talk to you about something and I need you to be completely honest with me. Okay?"

"Yes, mommy."

"You know what it means for someone to have a girlfriend or a boyfriend, right?" Hannah began.

"Um hmm, Stacey says that Joey is her boyfriend, but I think that's gross." Maddie said.

"Well, they are kids, so maybe that's why it's gross. What would you think if mommy had a boyfriend?" Hannah asked.

"Well, I don't know, I think it would kind of matter who it was." Maddie said with all honesty.

"Riley" Hannah said.

"Oh, mommy! Riley would be the best boyfriend ever. He's so much fun and he's my bestest friend. He likes the same pizza as me and he watches Moana with me and doesn't even mind when I hold him during the scary parts."

"So, you would be okay with mommy dating Riley." Hannah wanted to make sure.

"Yes, mommy, I am."

"What would you think about us staying at Riley's house for a while so that we can all get to know each other better?" Hannah asked.

"Will I have a bedroom of my own?" Maddie asked.

"Yes, you get a bedroom of your own. Riley even said you could pick out the bedding and decorations." Hannah said. Maddie looked a little sad, so Hannah continued, "If you don't want to, that's totally fine, Maddie, we can stay with Sophie and Bryan a little longer or we can go back home to our house." Hannah would swallow her fear the best she could if her daughter wanted to go back home. She would figure it out one way or another.

"I just miss my toys, mommy. I only packed some of them when we went to Sophie's house." Maddie said sadly.

"Oh, well, we would be moving all of our stuff to Riley's house for now. Not the couch and all that, because Riley has his own, but all of our clothes and toys. And if you don't want new bed stuff, we can bring your old stuff." Hannah explained. "I want us to stay here long enough that we can all decide if we want to be a family someday Maddie. But, if it doesn't feel okay, we'll go back home." By this time, they had arrived at Riley's house.

"Whose house is this mommy?" Maddie asked as they pulled into Riley's driveway.

"Well, it's Riley's and if you're okay with it, it will be ours for at least a while." Hannah said putting the car in park. Riley had told her he would leave the front door unlocked and he would be in the backyard so that she could show the house to Maddie before she saw the things he had bought for the yard. "Let's at least go take a look, okay?"

Maddie got out of the car and said, "This is a big house, mommy. Not as big as Sophie's, but way bigger than ours." No matter how long they had stayed, the house was always Sophie's and Bryan had no part in ownership as far as Maddie had acted.

"It is, and it has a backyard too. But I want to show you the house before we see the yard." She walked in the house and gave Maddie the tour. "This would be your bedroom, Maddie, like I said, Riley wants you to make it however you want it to be. Right now, it's just a pretty empty room because you get to bring your old stuff or pick out new stuff."

"Where's your and Riley's room, mommy?" the little girl asked as if she just assumed they would sleep together.

"Well," Hannah said walking down the hall, "This is Riley's room."

"But aren't you going to stay with him, mommy? That's what Sophie and Bryan do." she stated vey matter of fact.

"Well, do you think it's okay for mommy to sleep in the same room as Riley?" Hannah asked. She was surprised that her daughter was so prepared for that, but she realized that she shouldn't be. They had been staying with Bryan and Sophie for a few weeks and Maddie understood so much more than she sometimes gave her credit for.

"Yes, mommy, if you're his girlfriend." Maddie said. "Do you think you and Riley will get married, mommy?"

"I don't know, Maddie, that's part of why I want to stay here, to see if we all feel like it's a good thing for all of us. That's why I want you to know that you can say no if you don't want to stay here. Or if we start staying here and you decide you don't want to keep staying, you tell me, and we'll figure it out. We don't have to live here for Riley to be my boyfriend."

"Okay, mommy." Maddie agreed. "Where's Riley?"

"He's out in the backyard waiting for us." Hannah stated. "He wanted you to see what he got for you."

"He got me a present?" Maddie asked excitedly.

"Well, not a present really, but if we are going to stay here, he wanted you to have some things that might be fun." Hannah said. They walked out the back door and Riley was sitting on the deck.

"Hi Maddie." He looked at Hannah to try to gauge how the conversation had gone so far.

"Hi Riley!" She ran to him and gave him a hug. "Mommy says you got things for me to play with."

Riley scooped her up began walking with her down the few steps into the yard. He was surprised she hadn't already spotted the play structure, but apparently; she had been looking for him and that had been where her focus remained. But now she was looking right at the backyard full of things to entertain a small child and an army of her friends if she invited them over. It was Fall, so that meant the pool was closed for the year, but the rest could be used.

"You got these for me?" She said wide eyed.

"Well, the swimming pool has been here for a long time, but I got the trampoline and swing set for you." Riley said. He sat her down and she immediately ran to climb the play structure all the way to the top where there was a large platform that was pretty much the same as a tree house would be. She looked down and all around the yard. "This whole yard is for me to play in?"

"All of it, but not in the trees. Riley's going to put up a fence so you know where you can go, but until it's up, you have to stay close to the house. There are animals in the woods, not big scary ones, but when I was here the other day checking it out, we saw a fox, so we don't want you to go too close." Hannah explained.

"Okay mommy." Maddie said.

Riley walked back to Hannah's side and put his arm around her waist. It was the first time they had really shown any physical connection with Maddie close by and it felt right. "I was wondering if you wanted to plan to have Maddie's birthday party here?" Riley asked.

"I hadn't thought about that. There's been so much going on. I usually let her have a friend or two over because space is limited. And then we have a dinner with my family." Hannah seemed retrospective.

"Well, I haven't met your family. I don't know if you want that to happen at Maddie's party or if you want to handle it another way. But we definitely have the space here to handle it however you want it to go." Riley said.

"It's a month away, I'll think about it and decide in a couple of weeks." Hannah said. Then she got really quiet for a long time like she was deep in thought.

After several long minutes had gone by, Riley said "What is it, sweetheart, I can tell somethings on your mind. If you aren't ready for me to meet your family or you aren't okay with them knowing that you're living here, I'm sure we can work something out."

"No, that's kind of the point, I guess." Hannah said. "You haven't met my family, not a single one of them and you've been in my life for months now. You would think by now one of them would have stopped by or invited me over. Ever since the things has happened to Maddie, they've sort of distanced themselves. At first, I thought it was just that they weren't really sure how to approach it, but now, I just think they didn't want to get involved in a scandal. My parents aren't rich, but they do have a sort of standing in their church community and I don't know if they think I did something wrong and that's what caused the situation with Maddie or if they just don't want to acknowledge it. I know they wouldn't approve of us living with you. But I guess I'm at the point where I realized it's my life and I have to live it in a way that makes me happy, regardless of what they may think. It's not like we've been close for a while now."

Riley just let her talk, he didn't interrupt her and even after she was done, he could tell she was processing a lot. Finally, he pulled her closer to him and said "Hannah, I learned a long time ago that family isn't always blood and you make your family where you find love and support. When my parents died, Pops stepped in and became family for us. I know my siblings already consider you like family. I'm sorry that your actual family can't see what they are missing out on by not being close to you and Maddie, but it's their loss."

"I know, I just don't know if Maddie will be okay with them not being at her party." Hannah said sadly.

"Well, I have a feeling that she won't even notice if we do things the right way." Riley said. "She'll be too busy enjoying the people that do come to notice the people that don't."

"I'm sure you're right. And she's old enough and smart enough for me to explain that while they will always be our family, if they don't want to be a part of our lives, we can't make them." Hannah said.

"Speaking of her birthday." Riley said quietly. "What would you think of getting her a puppy?"

Hannah smiled, "I think you're going to spoil her."

"Well, she did ask me if she could have one sometime and we definitely have a big enough house and yard for one." Riley said. "Besides, I really like dogs." He took Hannah's hand and walked them over to the trampoline. "Hey Maddie, come here, I want to show you something."

The little girl walked to the side of the trampoline and Riley set her on the edge, he took off her shoes and did the same for Hannah. He pulled his shoes up and climbed on with them. "This trampoline is made to hold several people. We can all jump together." He took Hannah's hand on one side and Maddie's hand on the other then mother and daughter completed the circle. Riley began a low bounce because he knew with his weight, he could throw Maddie completely off of her feet. He wanted her to set the pace on how fast and how high they bounced.

Maddie varied between standing with the and jumping and sitting down and letting them bounce her like she was a piece of popcorn in a hot pan. Her laughter was infectious, and they were all having so much fun they barely realized that it was getting late in the day, and they hadn't eaten anything for hours. Finally, Riley said "What would you ladies think of running out for pizza and then getting your stuff from Bryan's house so we can spend the night here tonight?" If Hannah or Maddie weren't ready to move, he would be okay with that, but he hoped they would be.

"Yeah!" Maddie yelled, "Pizza!"

"Well, I guess that's a plan then." Hannah said laughing.

They went to Riley's favorite pizza place and got Maddie's favorite pizza. On the way to pick up their things, Maddie said "I still want to get my toys from our house sometime, mommy."

"We will sweetheart." Hannah said, "Sometime soon."

Riley had not missed the pale that had come to Hannah's face. "How about I take you over there tomorrow Maddie and we can get whatever you want to bring with you. And if you need anything for your room, we can go to the store to get that too."

"Can I mommy?" she asked.

"Of course, Riley has the key to the house so he can help you carry anything you want to bring." Hannah looked at Riley and she knew he had done that for her. He knew she wasn't ready to go back to that house yet and he was stepping in and making it, so she didn't have to. She hoped he could read the gratitude on her face because this man was the most amazing man in the world.

Chapter Twenty-One

Over the course of a month, Hannah and Maddie's things had all been gradually moved to Riley's house. She didn't know for sure when he had done it, but he had Sophie and Summer help him gather all of the personal items from the house. She hadn't had to go back there for anything. From what she could tell by what all was now in Riley's house, the only things left there were things that she didn't care about at all, pots and pans, furniture, nothing that would be needed as long as she was living in Riley's house. And she was pretty sure that she wanted to stay here forever.

It was the day of Maddie's birthday party and all of Riley's family was there including Pops and his wife. She also had several of her friends from school. She had gotten more things than any nine year old girl could possibly need. That was what happened when you suddenly became the only child in a family that was close knit and wanted to give her the world. Riley and Hannah had decided to give her a puppy, but they didn't want to do it on a day where there was a house full of people and they wanted her to have a say in which one they got so that would happen in a few days.

Riley did have a surprise up his sleeve though, but it wasn't for Maddie, although she was totally in on it. After all of her presents had been unwrapped and played with, and the school friends had all been picked up, Maddie 'found' a present that had been missed.

"Mommy, here's another present." Maddie said, playing her part perfectly.

"Did you miss one? Where did you find it?" Hannah asked puzzled. She didn't recognize the box as being anything she had wrapped, nor did she remember seeing anyone bring it with them to the party.

"I found it over there, but this one is for you, mommy." Maddie said innocently.

"Why would there be a present for me?" Hannah was totally baffled.

"I don't know, but you should sit over here and unwrap it so we can all see it." Maddie stated, pointing to a chair near the center of the deck.

Hannah sat down and began unwrapping the gift. She was puzzled as to why there would be anything for her at Maddie's party. When she got the box open, there was a beautiful bouquet of flowers inside. She pulled them out and held them to her nose to inhale the wonderful fragrance. She closed her eyes and just relished in the beautiful scent.

"Mommy, look!" Maddie exclaimed.

Hannah opened her eyes and Riley was in front of her on one knee with a small velvet box in his hand. She was pretty sure she knew what this meant.

Riley took her hand in his and said "Hannah, ever since that day I rode my motorcycle up to your house for the first time, I've been falling more and more in love with you and Maddie. When the two of you moved in here, it felt so right for us all to be together. I want the three of us to be together forever. I want to marry you, but I'm in no rush." He gave a small laugh and said, "Well, I'm in a huge rush because I want to be a family, but I will be patient until you're ready. Maddie and I sat down and had a long talk and I asked her if she would be okay with me asking you to marry me. She says she wants that." He glanced to Hannah's side where Maddie was standing, and she had the biggest smile and was nodding in agreement to everything he was saying. "So, Hannah," he popped the ring box open, and Hannah saw the most beautiful ring she had ever seen. It wasn't huge, it was practical, but it was beautiful a diamond with amethysts on each side, her favorite gemstone. Riley continued, "Will you marry me? I'm willing to wait for whatever date you feel comfortable with."

Hannah had tears in her eyes. This beautiful man who had shown her love and kindness and had given her joy and protection every moment since she had met him wanted to marry her. She glanced briefly at Maddie, just to be sure, but the look of hope and expectation on her daughter's face told her everything she needed to know. Maddie was completely on board with them getting married. "Yes, Riley, I'll marry you." She held out her hand for him to place the ring on her finger. After it was on, he pulled her to him for a long kiss.

"I promise I'll do everything I can to love and protect you and Maddie for the rest of our lives." Riley said.

"I don't doubt that at all, Riley. You've already proven it to me."

Maddie had totally been in on that surprise, but Riley had one more up his sleeve. Bryan handed him a small box and he turned to Maddie. He handed her the box and stayed down on one knee so that he was at her eye level.

"Another birthday present?" Maddie asked excitedly.

"Not really, this one's a just because present." Riley explained.

Maddie opened the box and there was a stuffed puppy inside. She pulled it to her in a big hug then she gave Riley just as big of a hug. "I love it Riley, thank you!"

"Well, that's just a promise of things to come, Maddie." He said setting her on his knee. "Your mom and I talked about it and we're going to get you a real puppy, but we want you to be able to help pick it out. But I have a question for you and if you don't understand or you're not ready to answer, that's completely okay."

The little girl nodded looking at him very seriously.

"I would like to have one of our friends, like maybe Jeremy over there fill out paperwork so that I can adopt you. If it's okay with you and your mom, I'd like to legally be your daddy. I don't ever want to replace your memories of your real dad, but I hope that I can be a good fill in since he had to go to heaven." Riley said. He had heard her during her bedtime prayers sometimes ask God to say hi to her daddy.

Maddie's eyes got as big as saucers, and she wrapped her arms around his neck and held him tight. "I want that too Riley, I want you to be my daddy."

Riley looked at Hannah to make sure that she was okay with that plan too and she had tears streaming down her face. He raised his eyebrows in question but instead of answering, she got out of her chair and threw herself into the family hug.

Everyone helped clean up from the party and they soon said their goodbyes to all of their guests and every member of Riley's family welcomed both Hannah and Maddie to their family. At first, Hannah cautioned that they weren't married yet, but everyone just assured her that was only a formality, she and her daughter were family already. During the time that she and Riley had been together, she had talked to Pops a few times and had told him some of her back story with her family. When he and his wife left, he leaned down and kissed Hannah on the cheek and softly whispered "If you decide that you don't want to invite your family, I would be honored to give the bride away. But please don't feel bad if there is someone else you would choose."

Hannah was kind of choked up that the man would make that offer, but she didn't know what to say at that point, the whole idea of marrying Riley was still so new to her. She thanked him for his offer. Sophie had told her that if she needed any help planning the wedding to let her know. Summer had made the same offer. Both Bryan and Trevor had told her to let them know if their brother ever screwed up and they would come and set him straight. All in all, she felt like they all saw her as family already.

They promised Maddie that they would start the search for the perfect puppy in the morning, but only if she went to bed without complaint. It ended up not being much of a problem though because her day had been exhausting for her. She hadn't stopped running or playing the entire day. Her friends were all envious of the huge backyard, which was now fenced in, but with a chain link fence so they could still see the animals in the woods. They had loved her trampoline because they could all jump on it together, and the play structure made an awesome fort for all of them. The only downside was that it was too cold to swim, and the pool had been closed up for the year. But Riley promised they could come back sometime when it was open the following Summer.

Once Maddie had gotten ready for bed, she said her usual bedtime prayer. But this time, she prayed for all of her extended family and friends as usual, she prayed for her mommy, and she prayed for her soon to be new daddy. Riley was so amazed at the love these two had for him and he loved them just as much in return. Maddie was practically asleep before her head hit the pillow.

Riley and Hannah made their way back down to the living room and sat on the couch. Riley pulled her to him and said "Sweetheart, like I said when I proposed, there's no pressure from me to set a date, but I very much want to be married to you sooner rather than later." He bent his head down to kiss her.

"I know Riley and really, I am not planning for it to have to be some big, huge affair. I'll get with Sophie, and we can start planning it. I really just want family and friends with us to celebrate the day. Although I don't know if any of my family will come and that bothers me a lot less than I would have thought it would a few months ago. Your family has welcomed Maddie and I beyond what I could have hoped for. Even Pops offered to give me away if my family isn't involved."

Riley scooped her into his lap and began kissing her more deeply. "Whatever makes you happy sweetheart."

"I think I would be very happy if you took me downstairs." Hannah said wrapping her arms around his neck.

"Downstairs, are you sure?" he asked. They hadn't gone downstairs since Maddie had been living here.

"I'm sure Riley. I am pretty sure Maddie is down for the count and I have told her that if she ever can't find us, to try knocking on that door. I haven't explained what's in there of course, I just told her it's a room for grownups, but she can knock on that door if she can't find us." Hannah explained. "It's been too long since we were down there.

She did not have to tell Riley twice, if she was sure she wanted to go downstairs and play, then that was exactly what they were going to do. He stood up with ease keeping her in his arms as he made his way to the basement. He put her on her feet long enough for him to get the key out of his pocket and unlock the door, but he scooped her right back up as soon as that was done. He carried her to the padded table and sat her on the edge. He went back to lock the door just in case Maddie woke up. By the time he turned back around, Hannah had pulled her shirt over her head and tossed it on the table beside the small couch. "Is someone anxious, sweetheart?" he asked.

"Definitely." she replied with a smile.

"Well, then we'll have to see what we can do to teach you some patience." Riley said taking one wrist and using the soft rope to tie it down to the ring in the center of the top edge of the table. He took the other wrist and tied it to the same ring. Her lower body was still fully dressed and able to move, for now. He put the blindfold on her and went to gather his implements of torture for the first part of their evening. A feather, a strip of sandpaper, a wire brush, and a piece of rabbit fur. He moved her down the table so that her arms were in effect, tied above her head. He used the feather to trace a light pattern up and down her arms, across her torso and under her breasts.

"That tickles, Riley." She said giggling.

"It's supposed to, sweetheart." Riley said. "But I think we need to fix another issue." He got a soft cloth and tied it around her mouth, effectively gagging her. He knew she wouldn't need a safe word for what he was about to do. Other than maybe drive her a little crazy, he wasn't going to do anything harmful to her. Then he took the sandpaper and grazed it over her skin, enough to be scratchy but not hard enough to leave any abrasions. She flinched often at the rough sensation. He alternated back to the feather lightly running all over her upper body and teasing her taut nipples with it, they peaked even harder with the attention he was giving them. He then changed to the wire brush, again, it was a scrape that was enough to be felt, but never enough to do any damage. With the wire, he was very gentle anytime he came close to her nipples or the tender flesh of her breasts. He could go a little rougher on her arms and shoulders. After her entire body was covered with pale scratch marks, he put the brush down and picked up the rabbit fur. He rubbed it all over her body soothing the scratches. He loved watching her body's different reactions to the sensations, she would go from wiggling from the tickle, to flinching a little with the sandpaper, back and forth between tender and rough put every nerve ending on alert, she never knew what to expect next. It was definitely a way to get her full attention to be focused on him and on what he was doing to her body. He could hear the changes in her breathing too, from slow deep relaxing breaths to sharp inhales and more of a panting sound. But it was time to move on.

    Hannah felt like her head was spinning, with all of the changes in sensation while being blindfolded, it was definitely a mind trip as well as making her entire upper body feel like one giant nerve ending. She felt Riley removing her shorts and her panties and then he flipped her over, so she was fully naked and on her stomach. She heard him walk over to the cabinet where he kept most of his floggers and other implements, and she thought she heard him open the refrigerator, which seemed odd, but he kept bottles of water in there for them to drink if they were overly heated from their sessions or love making. Maybe he was just getting a drink real quick.

    Riley started hitting her upper thighs and ass with a fairly hard thud type hit. It was a wide flogger with heavy elk skin falls. The hits could cover a wide area in a short amount of time. It wasn't long before he could tell that she was a little bit like a drunk person from the endorphins that her body was releasing from the pain. Her skin was quickly heated from the hard hits of the heavy falls. She was turning a deep pink and when he touched her skin with his hand it was on fire. Exactly what how he needed it to be. He took an ice cube from the glass he had filled out of the small freezer and began tracing it over her heated flesh. When the ice first touched her, she tried to let out a scream, fortunately, the cloth helped to dull the sound. Riley knew it hadn't been pain, but it was pure shock. He traced circles and swirls all over her flesh, quickly cooling it down from the heat of the flogger. She started to give a bit of a shiver when the heat was gone, and the cold fully began setting in so that was Riley's cue to move on to the next step in the process. He pulled the big soft Sherpa blanket from the back of the couch and laid it over her. He removed his clothing and cuddled up beside her. He removed the gag and the blindfold before untying her hands. Her eyes remained closed, and he was sure that her brain was still trying to process all of the sensations that she had gone through over the course of the last hour or so. When she finally opened her eyes, they were still a little glazed over. He smiled at her and said "Hi".

"Hi, I've never been on a roller coaster of sensations like that before it's a mind blowing experience." She said, still sounding a little groggy or spacey.

"I enjoy sensation play a lot." Riley said. "It's fun for me to watch your reactions to the different aspects."

"It was amazing, but I really want to make love to you now." Hannah said softly.

"I am all for that plan, but I want to carry you up to our bed and make love to you for hours." Riley said.

Hannah started to try to get up, but Riley stopped her. "I need to get dressed" she stated. "I don't want Maddie seeing me walk around naked or you either for that matter."

"I'll put on my pants; she's seen me without a shirt before. As for you, I'll wrap you up in this blanket and carry you up. If she sees us, she won't know you don't have clothes on. I can tell her you got sleepy so I'm putting you to bed." Riley said. "That's not a lie at all, you are a little sleepy."

"Okay, you sold me on the idea. I think my legs are pretty much mush anyway." Hannah said. She waited for Riley to open the door and engage the lock so that when the door closed, it would be secure. Then he came and scooped her up with the blanket wrapped securely around her. She pulled the door since he had his arms full of her and they made their way up the two flights of stairs.

They didn't see Maddie, but after laying Hannah on the bed, he said "I'll be right back, I'll go peek in on Maddie and make sure she's tucked in tight."

Hannah really loved how much Riley did to make the world okay for her and her daughter. She knew that if she hadn't ever wanted to go to the basement when Maddie was home, he would have respected that, but she loved their play as much as he did so she had begun preparing Maddie for the fact that they might be in that room sometime. They would be cautious, but she wasn't going to give up what she and Riley enjoyed.

Riley came back into their room. "She's sleeping peacefully." he assured. He took his pants back off and crawled into bed with Hannah and he proceeded to keep his promise of making love to her for hours.

Epilogue

One Year Later

Riley looked up when he heard the roar of a motorcycle pulling up to his house. He wasn't expecting anyone, but that didn't mean it couldn't be one of his brothers, or friends from BACA. The stature of the person getting off the bike didn't look familiar though, so he grabbed a rag to wipe his hands as he stood up to greet whoever the person was. Tala stood too, her tail wagging. She was generally always happy to see a visitor as long as they didn't seem to pose a threat.

He walked toward the motorcycle as the man took off his helmet and sat it on the seat. When he turned to walk toward Riley, he seemed familiar, but Riley couldn't place it. "Riley?" the man asked intrepidly.

"Yeah, I'm Riley, who are you?" he asked.

"It's me, Nate." he was hesitant, like he wasn't sure Riley would remember him.

"Oh, my God, Nate?" He put out a hand for a handshake but drew the man into a one arm hug that then turned into a pat on the back. "I thought you were dead man. When they shipped me home, I hadn't heard any other word other than you were MIA presumed dead. How'd you find me?"

"Yeah, they didn't find me for several weeks." he stated. "I stopped by Triskelion. I knew your brothers were trying to start it up when we were over there. They told me where to find you. Looks like you guys have a pretty good operation there."

"Damn, man what happened." Riley asked, "Wait, I have a feeling this is a story best told over a good beer. You want to follow me to a microbrewery not far from here. I know the owners. We have lots to talk about."

"Sure, sounds good." Nate agreed.
"First, let me introduce you to my wife and little girl."

"You have a little girl dude?" Nate asked with disbelief.
"Adopted, but yeah. Come on in for a minute." he said. As they walked into the house, Riley noticed that Nate had a limp. He would find out about that when they had a chance to talk openly. Riley called out, "Hannah, Maddie, come meet someone."

When they were in the living room, Riley said, "Nate, this is Hannah, my wife, and this is Maddie, our daughter."

"Nate, the one you told me about?" Hannah asked. At Riley's nod, she stepped forward and wrapped her arms around the man. "I don't know what happened, but I am so glad to know you are here. Riley told me about that last mission. I am happy you made it out."

"Thank you." Nate seemed a little awkward talking about it.

"Hi. Were you in the Marines with my daddy?" Maddie asked.

"I was." Nate responded.

"It's nice to meet you." Maddie shook his hand and gave him a big smile.
"I invited him to go with me down to the brewery. We have a lot to catch up on." Riley said. "If you don't mind."
"Not at all, I know you have a lot to talk about." Hannah offered.
"Just let me know if you're going to be here for dinner or if you are eating there." She gave him a kiss and turned to take Maddie back to wherever they had been before Riley called them to come out.

"You ready?" Riley asked. They both got on their bikes and took off.

Ten minutes later, as they were seated at a table at Five Sloths, Nate asked "Five Sloths, kind of an odd name."

"Yeah, there's a whole story behind it, but my sister is married to one of the owners."

"Summer is married, it doesn't seem possible that it's been so long." Nate said.
A waitress took their order and then Riley continued. "Yeah, she has her own tattoo shop right next to Triskelion."

"Speaking of Triskelion, it's a class act, man. Looks like you've been very successful." Nate said.

"Yeah, the shop does pretty well, and we do some PI and bodyguard type work on the side." Riley explained. "What about you man, where are you living, what do you do?"

"I live in Florida. I work for a private security firm. Most of the team are former military from one branch or another. You remember Major Curtis?" Riley nodded so he continued. He was the one who found me and helped me get back on my feet. An old friend of his opened a security firm down in West Palm Beach and offered me a job. He helped me get a place and helped a lot with my rehab, so I took it, I figured I owed him and it's what I know. You can take the boy out of the military, but you can't take the military training out of the boy you know?"

"Yeah, that's exactly why we do the side gig. It's what we know." Riley agreed. "So, what happened that day? I was walking out with one of the little girls, and I heard the implosion behind me. Before I could register what, it was, I was hit with a bunch of debris and shrapnel. I looked back and the building was literally a pile of rubble. They said they sent in troops and almost everyone was found except you. They assumed you were in one of the places that was too unsteady to search."

"Yeah, well, I had to take a leak, stupid of me I know, but I had drunk a ton of coffee to be awake, you know night missions were never my strong suit. Anyway, I was just coming out from behind the tree, and I looked at the building. It looked off, like it was vibrating or something. I don't know, it was milliseconds, but it just looked wrong, so I took off running to hide behind a rock. When the building came down, I wasn't sure if it had been hit by someone who was still there or if it had been set to trigger. I waited behind that rock for what seemed like forever waiting, listening, watching. But there was nothing man and I didn't want to stay around too long if the enemy was there. I got as close as I could without being too close incase another explosion went off and waited a few more minutes, but I didn't see anyone moving. You must have been on the other side of the building because I didn't see you. Anyway, I started running away from the building, but it was so dark that I couldn't see all of the debris. I either tripped over something or some debris hit me. I ran for a while before I realized my leg was on fire. I looked down and I could tell it was wet. It was dark, but I knew it had to be blood. I got as far away as I could before I passed out. I woke up, best I can figure several days later in a small home. They were friendlies, but they didn't speak English and I don't speak Arabic. They cared for my wound as best as they could in a dirt floor hut and fed me and all that. I had a pretty bad gash on my leg and a lump on my head. I must have gotten that when I passed out. Hell, I don't even know. A local doctor came in and checked me out and said it wasn't a good idea to try to move me until the lump went down. So, I stayed there until he felt it was safe for me to move. They got a message through, and a medic came and took me back to the base and then I got transferred to the military hospital. My leg had to be amputated a little below the knee. I asked if anyone else had gotten out and for a long time, they didn't say much about it. Finally, I found out everyone else was dead and you were back in Germany headed for the states."

"Why didn't you look me up sooner?" Riley asked, "Or at least call."

"That's part of what they helped me with. I felt like if I hadn't gone to hit a tree, maybe I could have helped someone or maybe I should have gone down with the rest of them. I had a lot of guilt to deal with. Major Curtis got me some counseling and help with PTSD. When I got to where I could walk again, he sent me to his friend Davis Kelly in Florida. He has lots of guys who have been through shit like mine, some even worse. I'm finally in a good place again so I figured it was time to find you and get it all out there." Nate said. "Riley, I am so sorry I wasn't in there with everybody, maybe I could have done something to help."

"Nah, man." Riley looked him in the eye. "It was rigged to blow once someone got deep into the building. They probably figured if someone had made it all the way in, most likely everyone else was at least inside. They knew we were coming. No one knows where they got the intel, but then again, no one ever does. There would have been nothing you could do. But I understand. For a long time, I thought I should have gone down with them too. It took a while and a lot of support from my family for me to realize that I had saved one little girl. If I hadn't been there that day or if I hadn't taken her out of there that minute, I found her we would both be dead."

"And now you're married and have a kid." Nate said. "It's awesome that you've done so well."

"Sounds like you're doing pretty good too." Riley stated.

"I am now." Nate began. "They bought a six story building and converted it. The first floor has a coffee shop and a couple of places to eat. They're open to the public, but it makes it easy for us to grab something too. The second and third floor are the business, the offices, and a gym. The top three floors were renovated into apartments. Any vet that needs a place can stay there for free until they can get back on their feet and if they are so inclined, they have a job if they want it."

"Sounds like a really great place." Riley said.

"It is, like I said, they got me out of my hole. They will hire anyone, regardless of their physical status. We have paraplegics and quadriplegics that work there. Some are completely whole physically but have damage you can't see. It doesn't matter, they find a place if you want one."

"I'm happy that you found your spot." Riley said. "I think until I met Hannah, I was kind of going through the motions. I worked as much as I could, but no matter how much I exhausted myself, I had nightmares, a lot. But I guess they're right when they say that the love of a good woman is a good thing."

They talked and reminisced for a long time. Riley invited him to stay at his house for a few days so that they could catch up. He had gotten a text from Hannah shortly after they had left saying that she was making sure the guest bedroom was ready just in case. God, he loved that woman, she and Maddie were his entire world.

THE END

Excerpt from Blazing -Triskelion Motorcycles
Book 1

Bryan stood slightly behind Pete. He didn't want to interfere with the reunion of the two siblings. He had been out of the military for years, but he still had the tendency of standing with his fingers interlaced behind his back, eyes forward, spine erect, shoulders slightly forward. It was how he tended to stand anytime he had to wait for someone or something. A few minutes later, he saw the young woman from the pictures in the file that lay open on his desk back at the shop. He had to admit, those pictures had captured her basic look, but they really hadn't fully done her justice. She was much more beautiful in person. She had a rich mahogany colored hair that was braided in a long tail down her back. She had sunglasses on, but he knew that she had eyes the color of light milk chocolate, he had gotten lost in them for several minutes at the office one day. Her skin was a pale olive color. He wasn't sure what her heritage was, but he would bet there was some Mediterranean connection in there somewhere, maybe Greek? By the time he pulled himself out of that whole wrong line of thinking, she was hugging her brother.

When Sophie pulled herself away from her brother, she noticed the mouthwatering piece of eye candy standing slightly back and off to the side. To be honest, she had noticed him yards ago as she approached, but she had told herself that there was no way this guy was with her brother. He was probably waiting for some girlfriend to get back from her latest trip to Maui or something. She hugged Pete and then asked, "Who is Hottie McHotterson there?" she said while using her chin to indicate Bryan.

Bryan had also been in the military long enough to have almost perfect hearing, and the character to not acknowledge that he had heard her statement. He just moved closer in position and politely waited for Pete to introduce them.

Pete just shook his head before telling his sister, "This is Bryan Lawson, your date for the party."

Bryan held out his hand and said "Ma'am" with a slight dip of his chin.

"Oh, god, don't call me Ma'am. That just makes me feel old and if you're my date, the last thing I want you thinking of me as is an old woman" Sophie said with a scowl.

"Not that kind of a date, Soph." Pete said shaking his head, "He's a trained bodyguard."

"Now why ever would I need a body…oh, you know." Sophie said.

"Yes, I know, and I think I probably know a lot more than you know." Pete stated irately.

Bryan kind of stepped between the two siblings, he had been doing that with his own family for years. Ever since their parents had died, Bryan had been the mediator and the one to keep them all together. "If I may, I believe this explanation is more suited for a private location and I think I might have a better way of explaining." He said looking between the two. Pete nodded agreement and Sophie just stood their stunned. Bryan put out an elbow for Sophie to take so he could direct them to the baggage claim area. After they picked up her bags, they went to a Starbucks in the airport and took their beverages to a more secluded group of chairs in the terminal.

"May I proceed now?" Bryan asked looking pointedly at Sophia.

"Sure, as long as you don't call me Ma'am again." Sophie said with sass.

"Thank you, Sophia." Bryan said with his deep 'no argument needed' voice. This woman was going to be a challenge. Not because he didn't like her sass and brashness, but because he did. He loved a woman with a bratty side, especially when he could be the one to spark that sass and then punish them for being a brat. Punish in only the sweetest of ways of course.

"She doesn't like to be called Sophia" Pete began.

"Oh, you hush, little brother" Sophia said with furrowed eyebrows. "As long as he doesn't call me Ma'am or some other old lady term, he can call me anything he wants." She turned her eyes toward Bryan and said, "Pardon my little brother's rudeness, you were saying?"

This woman was going to be the death of him, he had to remain professional. He was going to ask Trevor to put that on a repeating cycle of text messages to his phone. REMAIN PROFESSIONAL every thirty seconds or so should keep him out of trouble.

"Right, I was saying," Bryan began, "We have been keeping an eye out for Larry Ribinsky." Sophia's eyes immediately changed from light and flirtatious to serious and scared. "Pete hired my firm to run some facial recognition and things like that to see if we found him anywhere in this area. We also ran the same test for a one-hundred-mile radius of where you live. We didn't expect for him to be in Colorado, but we wanted to take precautions."

"And did you find him?" Sophia asked. She didn't know what she would do if he knew she was in Colorado. That had become her safe place.

"We did." Bryan confirmed. "He has been seen around your parent's mailbox on several occasions."

Sophia was puzzled, "Why would he be around the mailbox?"

"Hoping you mailed them something." Pete said somberly.

Sophia was just kind of sitting there staring at the floor with her arms wrapped around herself in a hug. How could he still be out there looking for her? Hadn't he done enough to ruin her life years ago? What did he want, another chance? That was never going to happen. She had hoped after he called the ambulance and went on the run, he would just disappear into some small backwoods' town in Oregon or Washington and live his life. She had always been worried that he would hurt another woman like he had her. But it wasn't like she would have been able to stop him from doing that. She might have been able to get him arrested, but her dad and her brother were attorneys so she knew not all bad guys went to jail, she also knew that even if they did, they got out eventually and they may take revenge on the person they thought put them in jail in the first place. "Why would he still be doing that? What does he want?" Sophia said softly.

"That's what we need to find out." Pete said. " And until we know, you have to have Bryan or one of his brothers with you at all times."

She looked to Bryan so he tried to give her a run down of how things would go. "You can't go to your parent's house, obviously. We don't know for sure if he keeps an eye on the house other than just checking the mailbox, but if he looks at the papers at all, he probably has a good idea that you might be in town. You're parents announced the marriage and celebration on the social pages and while I'm pretty sure Larry doesn't care much about most of what is on the social page, knowing who your parents are, he may be keeping an eye on it in case your parents post anything involving you. Pete suggested his friend Walt's home as a safe location for you to stay."

Sophia did not want to believe what she was hearing. That man had given her enough pain and torment in her life. She could not have him walking back in now, correction, she could not have him walking back into her life ever. She didn't realize she had sort of zoned out and sat shaking her head thinking of all the reasons that man needed to stay out of her life. She finally realized that she was not paying attention when she heard Bryan saying something.

"Sophia, it will be alright." Bryan was saying softly. "I promise you we won't let anyone hurt you. You have my promise that my siblings and I will do everything necessary to keep you safe from this man. He will not get withing ten feet of you."

Bryan sounded very sure of himself, and he and his team were probably very well trained, that didn't change the feeling of cold terror anytime she thought about Larry. She couldn't even think or hear his name without a chill running up her spine.

Pete had noticed the look of sheer terror on his sister's face. He still could only imagine what all that piece of scum had done to his sister. He knew what the hospital reports said, but he was sure they could only comment on the injuries that were fairly recent to when she had arrived. His sister had been with the man for months obviously there had been injuries that were healed prior to her stay in the hospital. The look of fear on her face told him that he had done the right thing. He needed her to stay as far away as possible while still allowing her to be here for the reception. He knew she really wanted to be here, and their mother would be disappointed if Sophie didn't make it. Their mother would understand, if Pete told her about Larry, but he was hoping to keep that piece of information away from them. The Lawson brothers were already taking care of checking his parent's mail and making sure he wasn't hanging around their house anymore. He just needed to keep her safe for a few days until she could make her way back to Colorado. His parents didn't need to know all of what Pete knew, although, he was planning to tell them that he had Bryan involved just in case her ex decided to try to make contact. He needed to make this seem a little less terrifying to her, somehow. "You remember Walt, right?" He asked, at her slight nod, he continued. "He's married now, to this really super sweet former ballet dancer. Her name is Rayne. They have a big five-bedroom home and they are looking forward to your visit. You won't believe this, but Zak has actually settled down too. He's not married, yet, but things are pretty serious between him and his girl, Skye. They got engaged at Christmas. I'm sure you'll meet them all soon. The guys are all looking forward to seeing you again." He wasn't going to say that they hadn't seen her since just after she got out of the hospital. She remembered that time as well as he did, talking about it would only give her more to think about and he needed her to move her focus from the past to the present.

    Bryan could tell that Sophia was getting lost in the past, and that would do no good for any of them. He needed to get her on the move so that she didn't have time to dwell on the past. The present needed to hold all her focus for the time being. He gave an imperceptible nod to Riley who would appear to be reading the paper to anyone that might pass by. What he was really doing was watching for any sign of the perpetrator in the general area. Trevor was outside in his truck with his computer running facial recognition scans on the feeds coming from the security system he had tapped into when they had arrived a few hours ago to get the lay of the land for the easiest path to get Sophia off the plane and into their truck. Riley tapped out a message on his phone and then gave a small nod back. Riley had sent a text to Trevor telling him it was time to pull up to the exit closest to their current location. It just so happened that the exit closest to them was a door that would normally sound an alarm if anyone opened it, so hopefully, Trevor had taken care of that too. "It's time for us to go" he stated simply.

"I'm not done with my coffee" Sophia complained.

"Then take it with you." Bryan issued the command in a way that would tell anyone that no argument would be tolerated. "It's time for us to go. Sophia, you need to learn to listen to everything I say and do as you are told. This isn't me trying to be some bossy arrogant prick. I'm doing what I have been trained to do to keep you safe. When I stand up, you will stand up. I will put my arm around you like we are a couple and we will head for that door over there." He gave a chin nod to the exit.

Sophia challenged him by asking "And how is setting off an alarm going to keep us from being noticed?"

"My brother has taken care of the alarm on the door, so that won't be an issue. Pete, you follow us out. Riley will be trailing behind us until we get outside." With that he stood up and fortunately, Sophia stood too. He put his arm around her, and they headed for the door.

Sophia wasn't sure exactly how she felt about Bryan. He came across as a bossy asshole, but he really did look good doing it and she had to admit, having his big muscular body pressed up against hers wasn't a bad thing at all.

Blazing: Triskelion Motorcycles 1
https://www.amazon.com/dp/173452796X/ref=cm_sw_r_cp_api_glt_fabc_J2Q7NQ2HQ198V4NAQ0ZK

About Robin Andrews

Robin Andrews still lives in the same small town that she grew up in. She began college headed for a legal career. While she still went into the legal arena, she set aside the idea of becoming an attorney for the much more rewarding life of a mother and grandmother. She has been married for almost thirty-seven years. She lives with her husband and her miniature Labradoodle, Hope.

She is the mother to three adult children (two boys, one girl) and grandmother to three grandchildren (two girls, one boy). She loves spending time with her family as well as trips to wineries on the Old Mission Peninsula in Michigan and the small Amish town of Shipshewana Indiana.

Her greatest joys in life are writing, reading and spending time cuddling with her grandkids.

Other books by Robin Andrews

Fallen Rayne (Five Sloths Brewing Book 1)
https://www.amazon.com/dp/B084KMZMKW/ref=cm_sw_r_cp_api_glt_1QZAR4RNNGCCS319R4PA

Opaque Skye (Five Sloths Brewing Book 2)
https://www.amazon.com/dp/B085B8B24P/ref=cm_sw_r_cp_api_glt_NJ9KY4X7Y3TXS95TPVR5

Encouraging Autumn (Five Sloths Brewing 3)
https://www.amazon.com/dp/B0893JH6TK/ref=cm_sw_r_cp_api_glt_Z6EF9BKQC45VXQK6NMBY

Resistant Summer (Five Sloths Brewing 4)
https://www.amazon.com/dp/B0971PDG1K/ref=cm_sw_r_cp_api_glt_ZGTVFT268TR6WAZ6TFTZ

Embracing Sunni (Five Sloths Brewing Book 5)

Coming Soon!

Blazing Triskelion Motorcycles Book 1

Blazing : Triskelion Motorcycles 1
https://www.amazon.com/dp/B08F78R8WG/ref=cm_sw_r_cp_api_glt_4X0F13G02SD92QFWEC1T

Sizzling Triskelion Motorcycles Book 3

Coming early 2022

Website: https://robinandrewsauthor1.wixsite.com/robinandrews

I would love to have you join my readers group on Facebook: Robin's Readers Nest.

https://www.facebook.com/groups/898899640504649/?ref=share

Made in the USA
Columbia, SC
23 December 2021